*The Death of My Brother Abel*

*Memoirs of an Anti-Semite*

*The Hussar*

*The Snows of Yesteryear*

# The Orient-Express

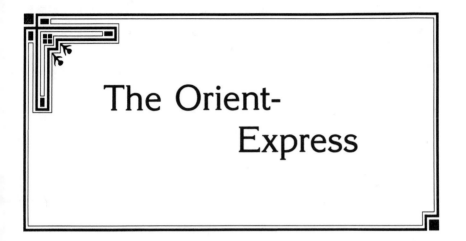

# The Orient-Express

Gregor von Rezzori

Alfred A. Knopf · New York · 1992

THIS IS A BORZOI BOOK
PUBLISHED BY ALFRED A. KNOPF, INC.

Copyright © 1992 by Alfred A. Knopf, Inc.
All rights reserved under International and Pan-American
Copyright Conventions. Published in the United States by
Alfred A. Knopf, Inc., New York, and simultaneously in Canada
by Random House of Canada Limited, Toronto.
Distributed by Random House, Inc., New York.

Originally published in 1986 in West Germany as *Kurze
Reise Ubern Langen Weg* by C. Bertelsmann Verlag GmbH,
Munich. Copyright © 1986 by C. Bertelsmann Verlag.

ISBN 0-394-57347-1
LC 92-52958

Manufactured in the United States of America

FIRST AMERICAN EDITION

# The Orient-Express

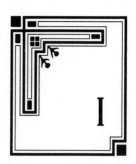

I

Nevermore! . . . *et puis, zut!*

VALÉRY LARBAUD

As he stood at the hall porter's desk waiting for his room key, he picked up the bulkiest of the brochures lying there, automatically, in the vacuum of his idleness, and because he'd made a habit of filling spare moments by reading something, no matter what: a page of any old book or newspaper or magazine, or any random leaflet—in a pinch he'd resort to the fine print on a medicine bottle. This was one of the many precautionary measures he had adopted to bridle his thoughts and prevent them from ending up somewhere unpleasant, reminding him of an insoluble situation or torturous memory. He dare not allow himself to slip completely out of the cage of reality, where until only recently he'd been held, to escape clothed in nothing but his naked humanity, and to risk encountering existence at every turn, divested of all the little fictions and illusions that made sleepwalking through life possible, guided only by experiences that brooked no deception and rendered him as sensitive as one who'd been skinned alive. Even the most asinine ads could be lifesavers.

## The Past Is Closing on His Heels

At first he merely ran his eye over the rich, glossy pages, provisionally as it were, before a more detailed reading later on; but this cursory glance sufficed to imprint indelibly in his mind the absurdly anachronistic scene depicted there: A string of midnight-blue, spanking-new sleeping cars boasting the words COMPAGNIE INTERNATIONALE DES WAGONS-LITS done in bold brass letters on their sides; they were drawn up at a spotless platform, lit with a hushed boudoir glow; conductors in uniforms as crisp as those of navy cadets stood with cap in hand, smiling easily as they bowed to models got up as ladies; in the background, fawned on by obsequious porters, a clutch of other travelers with hatboxes and other equally defunct pieces of luggage seemed straight from Madame Tussaud's; if one peeped through the gleaming windows of the restaurant car, one saw the glint of soft lights on cut-glass decanters and silver champagne buckets, and the waiters' geometrically stark black butterfly bows against chalk-white shirtfronts—in short, an unbelievable revival of a piece of the past, bursting with emotional meaning that once upon a time had formed the stylistic content of an epoch; but this ham-fisted rendition reduced it to a cheap parody. An abortive experiment attempted on an unworthy subject with inadequate means, as a lawyer might have summed it up, a vain endeavor to convey to a world sold on cheap criteria something that had once been sublime reality. The French, as usual, knew how to put it: *Prête-moi ton grand bruit, ta grande allure si douce, ton glissement nocturne à travers l'Europe illuminée, o train de luxe!* . . .

## . . . And So Is the Present

In an involuntary flush of sentimentality, which he quickly, vexedly quelled, he read the words VENICE–SIMPLON–ORIENT-EXPRESS in a garland of golden Art Deco foliage, and he suffered the worst attack yet of the impatience that had driven him from New York via San Francisco and Honolulu and Tokyo and Hong Kong and Bangkok and the devil knows what other festering human garbage heap tipped at the foot of towering concrete stalagmites, from one laminated plastic luxury hostelry to another, until he wound up here, in Venice.

Now he was standing in his room, exhausted from a morning spent worshipping at the myriad cultural shrines erected here to the glory of the "mussel-colored Queen of the Sea," trying to reassure himself with the personal effects laid out before him— the dressing gown, the paired hairbrushes in their leather case, the thriller on the bedside table, the tubes and phials of sleeping pills that he ever more readily used—that this was indeed his room. It was on the ground floor, separated by glass doors from a narrow terrace which but for a lushly verdant hedge would have overlooked the spacious courtyard with the inevitable pool; this was, in its noble dime-a-dozen design of obtrusive anonymity, referred to in the pathetic advertising blurb as "solidly superior." The wallpaper, the chrome pipes of the chairs, the synthetic upholstery of the bed and sofa, the curtains shielding the plate-glass window (beige and yellow, orange, lime-green and brown, tones that even in lighter shades absorbed dirt and had a cool, sobering effect while yet conspiring to create a controlled aesthetic coziness, here in the Mediterranean climate, to boot!)—the very calculatedness of the whole design was sickening.

## Subcutaneous Influence

The hotel catered to people with adventurous intimate tastes. The bathroom was constructed so one had a full view of it from the bedroom: a circular tub sunk into the tiled floor was surrounded by a transparent cylinder from floor to ceiling; it was easily surveyable from the suggestively broad double bed. One automatically projected the image of a sleek, naked female body wallowing juicily in a bubble bath or frolicking under a shower. A heavy ornamental mirror in an old-gold baroque frame was tilted toward the bed with a view to lending sluggish fantasies a helping hand, while the paper strips across the glasses and toilet seat thoughtfully dispelled hygienic misgivings. Hanging over the bed as a stylistically piquant extra was a reproduction of Botticelli's *Birth of Venus*, enhanced by the same kind of matte-gold ornamental frame as the mirror.

He saw it all, his eyes as expertly appraising as he was nauseated. Somewhere in his professional past he'd had to acquaint himself with the complex interests of a big hotel business, and he knew that these decorative effects were not determined by the findings of market research, as one might suppose, but rather came about all by themselves in the wondrous transition from the supposed to the actual anticipation of the customer's every wish. The respectability of the establishment naturally precluded comparisons with a bordello, yet it was perfectly clear that no one would move into quarters costing upward of four hundred fifty dollars a day all alone. Reflecting on how rationally to utilize such opulence led, in the minds of customer and creator alike, to images of a partner whose erotic finesse was commensurate with the rest of the peerless service rendered. The effect was to charge this excessively functional, germ-free, clinical atmosphere with the challenge of discreetly suggested but undeniable possibility. That this had an aphrodisiac effect surprised him not at all. Present-day psychology had acquainted almost everyone with the phenomenon of transference. Once, God alone knew how many moons before, he had had an affair with a young person whose narrow build and sparse secretions had necessitated the use of Vaseline; for years he had been unable to suppress the stirrings of an erection whenever he caught sight of a jar of that charitable jelly.

## Never Look for Yourself in a Looking Glass

What irritated him more than anything was the mirror. Its tilt, in that voluptuous baroque frame, was clearly meant to symbolize the grand maritime atmosphere of Venice, just as the juxtaposed Venus emerging from the oyster undoubtedly paid homage to D'Annunzio's "Queen of the Sea." But the mirror was neither dark nor flyblown, which would have made it reflect the diffuse, aqueous light of the lagoon city softly, with the

8

desired decorative effect; no, it was clear and bright, its reflections sharply outlined, a howling stylistic anomaly that he responded to as if personally challenged. With a fleeting sense of déjà vu (resulting—this much he knew—from an error in the interplay between the perception and storage-of-things-perceived mechanisms of his brain), he recalled a set of like circumstances he'd experienced long before and in like manner; it was as though fate were now demanding a pound of flesh for something he'd once bungled badly and then conveniently forgotten. This was a novel anxiety, and since he held his usual fears to be little more than hysterics, he told himself not to think about this one either.

But the call from the fog belt of his unconscious could not be ignored. It seemed to him that he was somehow being primed to receive a message, redeeming if painful, as though he had returned after a long and arduous journey to a devastated fatherland, where, although his house lay in ruins, it would receive him, as the last, ultimate place of rest: a condition free of fear and free of that persecution in which the wounding sharpness of his awareness had been exalted to a bright, transparent clarity. Yet he saw through the deceit of this promise, which seemed to him like an echo of all the impressions he'd gained since setting foot on European soil. It was only natural that the ghosts of the past should still be abroad here on this ruined and now unfamiliar continent, strewn with the remnants of familiar things—his own ghost, first and foremost—and that he, who had come to think of himself as his own ghost, felt trapped in a hall of mirrors.

## Once Upon a Time

He did his best, usually, to avoid mirrors. Of course the days were long gone since he'd thought, with growing despair, that he had ample grounds for evading his own reflection. At the tender age of twelve he'd been confronted with a true blossom of the Near East instead of the chunky blond champion he'd longed to see there, a rosy-cheeked Armenian lad whose upper lip was darkened by the hint of a brigand's moustache. He had never reconciled himself to this appearance, less and less when the delicate cheeks took on an olive tinge and the dark fluff of chin and upper lip became a dense blue-black growth that crunched beneath the razor's edge and could never be quite gotten rid of, even after the most merciless scraping. He still avoided mirror encounters when he could, and only rarely did his malicious delight in the treachery of his fate prompt him to take a look, finding an especially perfidious dispensation in the features of this ever more alien-looking acquaintance, whom for better or worse he was obliged to accept as himself. For whereas in the distant days of his youth—most especially during his school days in England—the unmistakable Levantine character-istics of his paternal forebears had made him suffer from much more than mere thwarted juvenile vanity, now, in his advancing years, when his appearance ceased to mean anything to him and when the folks back in his chosen home, America, scarcely ever reminded him that he was a foreigner, the likeness to his English mother was beginning to gain the upper hand. Once his peach-toned, oval Oriental face, with its precisely drawn, almost girl-ish eyebrows and virile, romantic shades about the full mouth, had made him as conspicuous among his flaxen-haired or gin-ger, freckled English schoolmates as a bird of paradise in a chicken coop. This had given way to a heavy, deeply scored, quite ordinary face, of a man in mature years with a solid crop of iron-gray hair, the head set powerfully on a muscled body of middle height; no one would suspect the fragile bone structure and smooth limbs of the Balkan prince of old. Only the large, disconcertingly bright, almond-shaped eyes hadn't changed; they still had an unsettling effect on women—perhaps more so now than ever—and an instinctively hostile one on men, not least of all himself.

So he didn't like to subject himself to a mirror's scrutiny, for it smacked too much of archaeology; every step he took in Europe seemed to bring him up against the walled-up wastes of

some outlived phase of his life, to recall the never wholly absorbed moods of the epoch of his youth, now being dragged out
and dusted off wherever he looked, dealing him a cruel spiritual
kick in the seat of his spiritually threadbare pants, so to speak.
Europe descended on him like the suddenly reactivated memory
of an old, unsettled debt. Things were going to be even more
unbearable here in Venice than they'd been elsewhere in the past
few weeks.

## Time Is Relative

He looked at his wristwatch. He'd lost his Omega, a trusty old
companion whose slender hands had swept the clear, white face
in tireless circumnavigation of the duodecimal cycle and reminded him constantly of its inevitable return, lost it under
shameful circumstances in a hotel in Honolulu. He suspected the
tiny, indigenous tart (in hula skirt and flower garland, no less)
he'd sent packing ere the dawn (so he could catch a few hours of
the sleep he'd lost in transit); the next day, at the Tokyo airport,
he replaced it provisionally with an eleven-dollar plastic chronometer.

Since then he'd needed his glasses to tell the time, for with the
farsightedness of age the weeny hopping black digits in the
silver-gray display window were hazy to the naked eye. He
didn't mind the extra bother; on the contrary, he rammed the
glasses onto his nose with a kind of masochistic *Schadenfreude*,
which was then automatically extended to everything else.
Nothing seemed to express better the transformation the world
had undergone in his own lifetime than this replacement of
hands circling imperturbably through the orbit of eternity with
the spastically fluttering phantom of ciphers caught in a
*perpetuum mobile* of assembly and obliteration, the last of
which pursued the second-by-second countdown of minutes'
and hours' decline into the nullity of the past with malignant
perplexity.

So now he was not content with just a single glance to ascertain the time, but dallied instead, observing with fascination how the smaller temporal units were snipped away from the bulk of the next higher, watching with childlike curiosity the freakish quadrille of sloping black rods: emerging and disappearing, nimbly bounding at the edges of the two squares placed one on top of the other to form a rectangle, combining to make the numerals from 1 to 9, disintegrating, and—at the very moment when an adjacent numeral was leaping into the next one higher up—beginning the game anew.

Long before, it would have been a matter of burning interest to him to discover how the thing worked (electronically and photochemically, needless to say), to build one himself, if he were able; but he'd abandoned such curiosity now. A man who sat on the boards of multinational electrical industries and chemical concerns couldn't afford to indulge in technical and scientific whims; one left science to the experts and its artful innovations to the consumers.

## ... Likewise Our Judgments

It tickled his sense of irony to think how easily this attitude could be construed as confirming the current views of the captains of capitalist industry, according to which directors of big companies needed little more for success than a healthy set of uncultivated impulses that nothing could divert from the essential—killer instincts. In commerce, as elsewhere, the essentials were elementary: danger lurking constantly on all sides, which required constant vigilance; the chance to make a killing, which had to be scented and sighted at lightning speed; the safeguarding of booty, which presupposed caution, foresight, and tact.

Thus, here too in the world of market-conscious technocrats—and above all in the world of their string-pullers, of whom he naively supposed himself to be one—everything depended on the possession of caveman survival skills. Researchers and scientists, the most brilliant minds of the age, poets, geniuses, and inventors were all being dictated to by troglodytes in charcoal-gray double-breasted suits beneath which beat cannibal hearts.

Very well, then! His own heart had little of the chilly stoniness generally ascribed to the cliché image of a money-maker; on the contrary, it resembled rather that of a rabbit—sensitive, vulnerable to a fault. He'd had to armor-plate it in order to become what he'd become; and he wouldn't have become that either, had fate ever offered him a choice.

## He Who Casts the First Stone

He'd been born into money, the son of wealthy parents, and he'd wanted to be a poet. It was only because he'd been flexible about his background and the mode of his departure from it that people thought his name could be found on the list of those who had the world on a string. He felt like the cobbler's son who has the makings of a virtuoso violinist but chooses to follow in his father's footsteps. Maybe his mistake was that he had become a damn good cobbler, including having grown a monstrous cobbler's thumb. What he'd been doing all his life was not his nature; over and over again during the past weeks he'd been amazed at how easily he'd shrugged off his professional past, all the intricacies of his ways of thinking and, with them, all feelings of responsibility, all temptations to rejoin the rat race. The presumed killer instincts were no longer functioning. The lion now wandered innocently among the lambs as though he'd never partaken of anything stronger than the meadows' morning dew.

He thought of the office he had left behind in Manhattan, and it was as if on leaving it he had closed the door forever on that part of world reality which was composed completely of superpowerful fictions. He wished he'd been as successful with the rest of his existence.

In the chronometer's display window, the numeral was leaping from 8:28:58 to 8:28:59. This was not the correct time, for he had never quite figured out how to reset this plastic watch and therefore still carried Tokyo time around with him, vying against his pulse. To find out what time it was here in Venice one had to subtract eight hours—or was it add? He wasn't sure, but somehow he almost always got it right. At the end of the next second, two zeros were momentarily profiled; then the right-hand one disintegrated and 8:29:01 came into view. In the first of the two possibilities for adjustment, this meant that one must replace the eight with a twelve, and this again, in the old manner of speaking, meant that it was nearly half past twelve, time to start thinking about lunch.

## You Can't Escape Your Memories

He wasn't hungry. Indeed, the mere thought of food revolted him. For the duration of a fluttering heartbeat he was seized by a fear that had dogged him on and off for weeks. Here in this room, in the umpteenth luxury flophouse of his aimless journey around the world, he'd been standing motionless for some several minutes, rooted to the spot, looking around himself like a scout in enemy territory. The cream-colored curtains were half drawn and the glass door to the inner courtyard stood open, as he'd directed; the heat didn't bother him. He was born in a country of climatic extremes, close by the languid waters of the Danube delta on the Black Sea. His childhood memories were rich in scorching summers whose evenings were screened as if in smoke by swarms of mosquitoes from the lagoons, rich in icy winters when snow crystals from the Dobrudja steppes came hurtling at his face like tiny stinging daggers. Later, when he'd been sent off to school in England and was obliged to do battle with his schoolmates (and part of himself) to the very limits of his body and soul, he'd been proud of his Spartan toughness and insensitivity to differences in temperature; even now he had retained this Boy Scout attribute, which caused distress to many women in his life, delicate creatures who, true to the spirit of the

14

age, liked to feign a shiver even on the warmest Riviera nights
in order to have a pretext for drawing a sinfully expensive pelt
across their naked shoulders. . . . *Comme la nuit les rend sages, et
comme elles se taignent bien! Et comme elles sont attentives à tous ces
regards blancs qui bougent dans les buis et les lauriers noirs!* . . .

He quickly gave his declamation a note of mock parody, but
didn't fool himself for an instant. He was irritated to have to
concede that yet another characteristic, till now heroically suppressed, filled the cliché image of the ruthless money-maker—
his proverbial sentimentality.

## Nor Can You Escape Your Idiosyncrasies

He allowed himself one small consolation: In his case sentimentality was, after all, a kind of cultural-critical sensitivity. The
epoch of his youth was as surely anchored in these visions from
his fantasy kitsch kitchen garden as it was in popular songs of
the period, or in the Art Deco medallions shown in the new
Orient-Express brochure. There was a private, personal side to
this, but also a general one; and if he now testily called himself
to order, it was not only on the grounds of self-defense, with
which he'd tried to master the emotional upheavals of the past
weeks (the desperately depressing doldrums of his marriage),
but above all because he hated the nostalgia that was now so
fashionable; in countless style-quotations, people were endeav-
oring to recapture the zeitgeist of the first decades of the century—as though those years had been more original and
harmonious than today's, had shown the world a more colorful,
richer life, a more vivacious, less abstract sense of the present.

## ... Nor Can You Recycle the Cycle

Such regressive yearnings probably conformed with a natural
enough feedback rhythm in the spiritual life of successive generations, but he couldn't shake the suspicion that here was a case

of willful forgery, that the repetition of these turgid motifs was occasioned, if not indeed sponsored, by the desire to up-value the few remaining cultural relics that had not as yet come up for auction in the selling of the West.

If he had been looking at this as a businessman, the thought could have left him cold, but somehow it touched an inner corner of him that had not yet frozen over. He rebelled against the cheap fancy-dress salesman trick to con him into believing that he could turn back the clock a half-century and experience—no, that the *world* could *re*experience—something that had been truly lost. The blindness to the period's stupendous nonfulfillment of promises, and to the innovative war cries that had gone along with this betrayal! This made him angry—as though just such chiliasm hadn't brought about the downfall of the Old World!

He had only once before revisited the old continent, shortly after the war, for he had an invincible, idiosyncratic objection to traveling. The debris of Europe's devastated cities and their gray humanity had erased all remnants of glitter from his memory. Since then, remembrance was painful. His memory wasn't drugged, as it seemed to be with others, but it tucked its tail between its legs. He balked at every confrontation with the past and was incensed by the masquerade in which today's media-washed mob tried to steal away from the present, which sold it no better a dream of the future than the questionable one of the state of the world a half-century before.

Cussedly, he declared himself content with every aspect of the present, above all its technology, which earned him good money. Still, he abhorred air conditioning, and now as he stood, listening carefully, there still lingered in the room something of the sterile icebox atmosphere that he'd sensed on arrival and promptly ordered turned off. Future soul-researchers might perhaps discover a link between this particular idiosyncrasy and the fact that he'd first experienced automatic room-temperature control (the very first in Europe, as far as he knew) in a Paris bordello, the Sphinx, an establishment to which he was deeply indebted for much valuable erotic education (read: character development).

But they'd be wrong. Even now, looking back critically, he could think of nothing in the comfort of the easily afforded and therefore carefree erotic pampering he received there that might have led to emotional hang-ups, no sign of any reason for a lasting aversion to the well-balanced room temperatures in which he had once performed his personality-forming exercises.

## Is There Mind Conditioning As Well?

He tended to believe that the roots of his distaste lay in the bronchitis he contracted in New York each July, when the discrepancy between the arctic temperature in offices, apartments, and restaurants and the tropical heat outdoors made excessive demands on the human body. His wife Linda's psychiatrist would not entertain so simple an explanation, of course. But then, he wasn't going to consult a shaman of soul research on the matter; his memories of the Sphinx were too valuable for him to risk exposing them to the probes of this most dubious of all newfangled sciences.

And then those stays in Paris to break the journeys (London–Paris–Bucharest–Braila, or Braila–Bucharest–Paris–London) had taken place in the last fairy-tale epoch of the *grands trains de luxe*, when the Old World life-style had already taken on that note of parody which facilitated its present renaissance, when everything that came from America had the irresistible freshness of innovation—jazz, bobbed hair, the Charleston. The Paris of Josephine Baker was one of the first American outposts that soon swept the continent and turned it inside out; paradoxically, air conditioning was born of the breezy, barbaric, carefree optimism that had transported European life expectancies. In the meantime, the clobbered century grew old. So much had happened to daunt the American dream and transform its promise

17

into the beginnings of genuine barbarism. And European decadence had an insidious, retroactive influence on the American myth; you could surmise an inherent Citizen Kane lurking in every shoeshine boy who made a million, not to mention the hybrid metastases of European thought—as, for instance, the teachings of Sigmund Freud (this was, by the way, one of the sorest abrasion points, on which his opinions clashed with those of his wife and her spiritual clan).

## The New Jerusalem

He loved America, but he was no longer lacking in skepticism about the American message of salvation. Although his business sense, solidly centered in political cynicism, went along with the tenet that the cheapest way to have social justice was to supply the world with fast food and uniform trashy clothing, he objected to the American notion that everyone had a right to demand the psychological key to each fellow human being's behavior pattern. The idea that for reasons of social responsibility he should owe the world an explanation for his aversion to air conditioning, for example, made him so angry that he didn't immediately notice what a dirty trick his imagination was playing on him: when all was said and done, no one was taking him to task—except perhaps the ghost of his wife, which had been clinging to him ever since he left New York so precipitately and even here majestically prompted other spooks that loomed up out of the garbage heaps of the past to dance in attendance before her.

He was tempted to step outside to escape this assault and spend the afternoon lying in a deck chair on his terrace. But the air would be thick with exhaust fumes from the *vaporetti;* also, he wanted to avoid the postcard magnificence of Venice for a while. If he had not felt at home in the corrupted Americanism of America, then even less so did he here in the Americanized antique-junk sale of a putrefied Europe.

## It's the Set That Makes the Play

He felt that he was witnessing a theatrical performance and that the director hadn't been able to decide where to set it: in Belle Époque Venice or in modern-day California. The lush, leathery, lacquered-looking foliage of the shrubbery outside his window might be plastic, as was almost everything else in this progressive hostelry for fugitives from the present—who were now out on Venice's canals and bridges, trying to escape their lack of direction by gulping down historical kitsch. The perfection of the small, salmon-colored blossoms also smacked of artifice. What stopped him from going out and checking was the sudden appearance of a white linen jacket with gold buttons in the fuzzy blue space between the splotches of green foliage: the heraldic insignia of a waiter on his way to the pool, balancing high above his shoulder, no doubt with dandyish vanity on extended fingertips, the usual tray of Negronis and Bellinis and the inevitable bowls of almonds and peanuts and cashews.

This was all he needed to fill in the picture of what was going on behind the bushes. In his mind's eye he saw the low, closely pruned box hedges around the lawn edging the flagstone-framed oblong of water; above, in the leaden light of the heat-hazed Venetian noon, were sprinkled umbrellas over chaises longues laden with roast-brown female flesh; he saw glistening oiled limbs and trunks; thighs and loins subjected to the cruel cut of bikini laces; flat bellies and dimpled navels above the fluffy foothills of pubic hair; breasts—weighty and broad, squashed and scrawny—of the legitimate or illegitimate traveling companions, laid out in rows on their fronts and backs, who compensated their consorts for the high prices of the rooms.

He imagined with agonizing clarity the glitter and gleam of their necklaces, bracelets, and rings; saw their blonde hair budding black at the roots, the dark, shining panes of their sunglasses reflecting iridescence, the sharp bloodred of lacquered toenails and fingernails, the lipstick traces they left wantonly on glass rims and straws, the cigarette cases and precious lighters, the oil-blotched fashion magazines and other trivial reading matter, the lotions, creams, scalp-massage brushes, eyedrops, Kleenex, and saccharin in plastic beach bags . . .

. . . and in the water the strident splashing children of a family of Latin American nomads, blithely spouting water like geysers as they emerged screaming from the pool, only to plunge back in from the diving board, holding their noses and tucking up their legs like monkeys . . .

. . . and a little apart, in a quiet backwater, immersed in big-business powwows as they trod water or hugged the edge of the pool within reach of their martini glasses, the remains of erstwhile hirsute glory slicked down in black and silvery rows across their shining pates like sardines, two or three of the substantial gentlemen whose silent checkbooks kept the wheels turning here—kept the lubricious epidermises suitably bronzed, the bellies bloated, the backs bedecked with noble boutique rags, the fingers, necks, and wrists jangling with brilliant baubles and beads—and ensured that the great money-gobbling engine idled away in neutral . . .

. . . while every now and then one of their wives' mahogany-brown Latin lovers got up from the grass, sauntered to the water's edge, and slid in like a salamander, a trail of bubbles behind him, to surface again after half a length, flicking off the water with a shake of his black-enameled locks and a flash of his white-enameled teeth.

## To the Skin of Our Teeth

It was all too familiar, too much his own world to tempt him. His knowledge of the environment was too exact; he could provide details on the spectacle with embarrassing precision. He could imagine the men out there down to their very hemorrhoids and prostate swellings, the women to their conscientiously checked ovaries; he knew about their heart pills, their stomach pills, their little liver pills; knew by heart the salt-free diets they observed to keep their blood pressure down and the macro guidelines they followed to keep their ideological spirits up and their bodies thin. He knew of their anxieties about stock market plunges and children hooked on drugs, he knew about the greed for wealth and social prestige that made them malicious, and he knew the incredible energy they invested in their efforts to keep the ailing splendor of New York, Los Angeles, Rio de Janeiro, London, and Paris alive. He saw them hectically killing lifetimes in their air-cooled offices, wheeling and dealing in their three-star chuckwagons, saw their wives being mummified with chemical mud at beauty parlors and gobbling snacks and gabbing between shopping sprees and analytical hours. He pictured them in tuxedos and haute-couture gowns at dissident-ballet evenings in New York and state receptions in Paris; and naked, with sweat-soaked clumps of hair on dripping chests, and thighs rampantly agape during the breathless, coronary-imperiled coitus of siesta time in penthouse suites or luxury dosshouses across three continents. . . .

## Tat T'wam Asi . . .

He didn't like to be reminded of his own existence. So he had little alternative but to resign himself to solitary confinement in this room, order a salt-free, low-calorie lunch, and take a little nap perhaps (no espresso in that case!). What might then follow—later in the afternoon, the evening, and the question of how to get through the insomnious hours of night—belonged to a distant future in which he mantically declined to intervene. After four weeks on the road he knew himself and his present condition well: any intention or plan might at a moment's notice be overruled in favor of some neurotic idea or hysterical whim. Whether his anxieties made him an even more sensitive bundle of nerves than usual or whether they were a byproduct of his neurosis was all one for the moment. In any event, he should keep quiet.

## Sex Is No Escape

He even lacked confidence in the one method that until now had proved most effective in inducing anesthesia, namely picking up some broad and blasting the awkward hours before dawn with the most soul-killing, thus most redemptive, of all activities. It wasn't the first time he'd fallen into *tedium vitae* with all its quicksands. He had learned that it was wiser, and tactically more successful, not to resist, not to panic, but instead calmly to surrender to his moods. He must rely on his perfidious skill at seeming to yield while tenaciously holding his ground—a quality that had doomed to failure the plottings of many a capricious lady who had kept him company along life's way. His proficiency was based on the safest of all speculations, that of time's healing power. With the passage of time, after all, most things seem to take care of themselves.

## D'you Hear the Death Knell?

It was just this thought that triggered what he wanted most to avoid thinking of. The idea that he would soon die was a fancy he rejected as infantile and lacking in taste, but it had nonetheless become a constricting certainty. The ridiculous fear that seized him, in spite of his valiant willpower, was not of agonizing suffering or of death itself, something he could imagine only vaguely. It was more a metaphysical constriction, a spiritual need, in a form he'd not experienced since his childhood except in nightmares.

No, it wasn't his death that haunted him; his no-longer-being-here-on-earth was an idea too abstract to be tangible. Even when he imagined his corpse, on its bed or in its coffin, it was no more than a black-and-silver embellishment of the gap he'd leave behind—rather like the lame old joke that the way to make a gun barrel was to take a hole and cast iron around it. Nor was it the macabre thought of decay, the decomposing of his somatic being into cesslike goo, a trite pile of ash—it wasn't this that stung him with the premonition of his impending end. Horror stories of graves and tombs were fine for frightening children, but not a sixty-five-year-old. Besides, the thought of a private world-crash, which individual death undoubtedly was, was mitigated by the not ludicrous possibility that it might coincide with or only just precede a more general, world-embracing perdition. That was one good thing about dying these days—one no longer need envy the bereaved.

## Life Is There to Be Lived

Yet not even the solace of this sentiment banished the deep disquietude into which the heightened awareness of his mortality drove him. Still, he had avoided like the plague—since his stormiest and most asinine younger days—any preoccupation with the ultimate purpose of his existence, no, of all existence, period.

That really did smack of pubescence, immaturity, dubious literature. He couldn't say exactly what it was that troubled him now, since nothing dire threatened him, thanks to his fundamental conviction that there was basically no purpose at all that had to be fulfilled. For a long time he'd been certain that life found its meaning in nothing other than itself, in existing, pure and simple. Life was there to be lived, that's all there was to it. Each person lived his own life—while five billion (or more?) crusted over the earth's surface like a plague of mites, worshipping many gods but serving only the Great Mammon. And if he could say of himself that he'd built his pile higher than most, that he'd served the idol most of them worshipped better, more exclusively, and more ruthlessly, and thereby been a more satisfactory minion (posterity in a communist-oriented world might take him to task on this, but certainly no Christian godhead or any other supreme celestial authority would), it didn't change the fact that he would expire along with the rest of the vast teeming mass of his contemporaries, just like countless generations before and innumerable ones after him. No one left traces on the grand scheme of expiration. In an operation of cosmic dimension and perpetual repetition, it was insane to ask questions as to the meaning and purpose of individual existence. There was the rub. Here lay the root of his anxiety.

## How to Make Friends

As a rule, he was spiritually elated when pondering such weighty matters; he experienced quite the opposite of the dread that journalists—first and foremost the stigmatized intellectuals from Linda's circle of friends—sought to inspire in readers and listeners. There was something cheering, consoling, in declaring the worthlessness of individual existence; all the arbitrarily established categories, all the ethical and moral Procrustean beds our civilizations held ready for us and onto which life never ever quite fitted; all meaning evaporated before this immeasurability. He even sensed something like a human bond in the common awareness of everyone's shared worthlessness and inestimability. He persuaded himself that such a credo entitled one to take a step up in civilization, humanism *ex ovo*, out of an egg, laid and hatched by no metaphysical hen.

## And How to Cope with Them

Opinions of this sort gained him little sympathy among the people whose ethics formed the guidelines for sales policy in the press and, consequently, for the mental and emotional attitudes of a broad and influential (because rich) sector of society. Linda was convinced that he simply liked to provoke her friends. But it was his honest belief that basically nothing counted, nothing one did or did not do, nothing one achieved or fell short of, far less what one believed or said. Imagine his dismay, then, on discovering that old, long-since-discarded values, tenets he had

24

believed dead and buried, were apparently still sufficiently alive to allow him to enjoy the coziness of nihilism.

Whenever the thought of imminent death came to him—and it came more and more often, at the most unexpected moments, isolated in time, and therefore with the character of manic inspiration—it released an avalanche of pangs of conscience. Not so much because of possible misdemeanors he might have committed against others (his self-assurance forbade him such flights of modesty) as because of the extent to which he had sinned against himself.

If one had to answer to some judge (ever present, of course—in oneself), then in a world addicted to performance it was a question of how well one had exploited one's initial capital. (At the back of his mind he remembered the distinction made by a German sociologist between ethics of conscience and ethics of responsibility.) He declined to brood over mistakes that, in spite of all he'd achieved, had meant he could not be at peace with himself; he knew his life was faulty in design. From childhood his dual nature had split him down the middle and he had never been able to put the pieces together. On the other hand, he regarded himself as the sum of two contrary components, and he wanted to subject this "persona," which of necessity he'd become, to the categorical imperative—one that complied with its inherent principles, needless to say. In this respect, he had every reason to be happy with himself.

## Spirit as an Enemy of the Soul

He could well imagine that his enemies (like all men of his professional cut he had many, with astounding differences of motive), not only Linda's friends but many others, were ready to charge him with a whole chain of misdemeanors against morals and ethics, here and there against valid laws, and even against the dignity of their own person. But they'd fall well short of the list he could cite himself, were he to discard the conviction that for him—a financier, a high priest of Mammon—a different set of rules applied. But this was merely drivel that pulp journalists favored—all those writers congregated around Linda, from book-producing salon philosophers and essayists pertly oriented to current ideologies to purveyors of dramatically moralistic newspaper and magazine articles, all of them trotting out dog-eared opinions *con brio*, as though they were revelations or confessions of faith—part of the unbelievable hodgepodge of pessimistic culture-drivel whose champions drove the inflation of the printed word into the realms of the absurd. They prated against the world's godlessness and soullessness, the disdain of science and the threat it constituted to Mother Nature, the idolatry of Mammon in the consumer society, and above all, against him and his like, the evil beneficiaries of evil times, the exploiters of humanity. They ranted against anything and everything, what had been and was and might ever be. And yet how cheap it was to stir one's literary soup over the flames of general disgust at the world's present condition! If things were indeed so far along that a hysterical reaction on the part of a head of state, or a miscalculation in the defense or attack mechanism of a major power, could trigger events in the course of which nothing remained that took note of the erstwhile existence of the whole zoological human species, or even the ability to recognize it as such—then surely the only worthy way to behave was to laugh or keep silent. But the boys continued earnestly to drivel on, gumming up the brains of the five-billion-headed, bipedal, swarming human race and denouncing (while sipping their whiskey) all those who were cynical enough to have a quick fish in this murky but still highly productive pond.

## Here He Stands, Empty-Handed

Even if he hadn't belonged to their ranks—which he did, of course—he wouldn't have bothered to deny or whitewash it for a second. It did not fall into the category of existentialist sins he accused himself of. Whatever it was that made him stray from the straight and narrow lay outside any banal moral codes and could be summarized as an offense against life's elementary laws; for instance, he couldn't come to terms with women, with women in general and with the one particular specimen who currently disturbed him most: his wife, Linda.

All his assumed cynicism and nihilism came to grief when confronted with Linda. Even his fatalistic speculations on the fugitive passage of time were ineffectual. He had been married to her for twenty years, and the more bitterly he tasted the transience of their days (it was the tiny, suddenly accumulating changes that brought it home to him most, the popping up of minute signs of wear and tear, like the numerical spooks in his Japanese wristwatch), the more clearly it emerged that he'd missed the real point of living and was continuing, hopelessly now, to do so. The final temporal curtain, which death would drop on everything, would not relieve his sense that, in spite of his performance (which was morally incommensurable in any case) and the delights of the game he'd played so hard, he'd gone out empty-handed.

It was this, laughably, that drove him around the globe as if acting out a junk-novel plot. One day some four weeks before (was it really that long?), he'd upped and left. "Suddenly the scales fell from his eyes: How shamefully and carelessly he'd allowed his life to drift." Since then he'd been on the road, "even more adrift in time and space, aimlessly and endlessly," as Linda's protégés might put it.

## Let's Be Fair

In this general conflict, nothing distinguished him from his consociates out there by the pool, except perhaps that they were less hysterical, had reconciled themselves to their calamities, and were sojourning here as well-installed summer holidaymakers, whereas he, in an attack of climacteric panic, had allowed himself the indulgence of "throwing off the bonds of convention" and had scurried off with his embezzlements like a petty book-maker (he remembered having read something of the sort by Hermann Hesse)—in other words, he'd done something he hadn't had the courage to do earlier. Would his life have been more purposeful if he had done it earlier? Now, in any event, it was much too late, therefore superfluous. For this reason alone he should have been ashamed.

Even more laughable was the circumstance that he, as a rebel against so-called established life (above all marriage), had landed right where he'd have landed as an obedient member of the flock, slap-bang in Venice. The constant thought of Linda made his stay here into a kind of negative of a honeymoon photo.

Yet perhaps there was a certain intrinsic value in the very gesture, in the childishly adventurous nature of his jailbreak, due less to its being a relapse into infantile spontaneity than to his awareness, as his soul's own assessor, that he readily despised his doubles sprawled around the pool for their listless compliance with the fatality of their existence.

## Love Your Neighbor As Yourself

No doubt he did them doubly wrong: they were way ahead of him not only with their cool heads and collected nerves but with their blank-eyed honesty and lack of pretension as well. On the occasions when they too oozed sentimentality about their screwed-up lives, they did it uninhibitedly, sometimes even elated at making a deep poetic vein gush freely. They too blabbered about their women, as though this would exonerate them from the guilt of unfulfilled existence. They too whined about not getting what they wanted from their women, even when the women were gracious enough to allow themselves to be bedded. There was no releasing these men from their solitary confinement. And yet they were primitive (or clever!) enough to leave it at a lament (or an accusation). They didn't work themselves up to considering the baffling truth that women were nothing but symbols, after all: embodiments of Eve—yes indeedy! delicious, palpable embodiments of the eternally unreachable, seductive, alive—fashioned from Adam's flank to show him how dense his flesh was, a prison that hopelessly entrapped him; to show him plastically—yes indeed! he could grasp it with his hands, touch it with his skin, taste it with his lips, smell it with his nostrils, see it with his eyes—how terminally imprisoned and alone he was in the jailhouse of his flesh. She was a sign posted to remind him that being damned to solitude was final and that release from prison could be effected only by death.

They too, his contemporaries out there beyond the too green, too shiny bushes with the too perfectly salmon-colored blossoms (his equals; slaves dangling at the end of the golden chains they tried to bind their women with), they too upbraided God, the world, and of course their women. But they did it from the security of an unshattered faith in the rectitude of their complaints, and they did not claim that there must be some way out, that if only it could be found, the dungeon-world would be gently and transparently clear.

## We Are All Sons of Mothers

It was not just this secret expectancy of a remission that made him feel so decisively superior. His pride came also from being able to say that his requirements were not those of a naturally needy person; he was not a beggar in matters erotic, but exactly the opposite. If his life's fulfillment had run afoul of women, to put it uncouthly, that was because he'd had too many of them rather than not enough.

Nurtured by women, he had learned at an early age to reap a healthy benefit from their competition for his favors—whether the rivalry arose between his English mother and his Armenian father's spinster sisters, or between his Romanian nurse and his German and French governesses, or between two or more concurrent mistresses. Like everyone wooed with bribes, he despised the wooers; like all spoiled people, he was raised to discontent. He demanded not only obedience but also the capacity to awaken love in himself. And since his demands precluded a facile accomplishment of the latter aim, he soon had more than enough of compliance.

Like all men pampered by women at an early age, he overestimated the value of manliness. In his adolescence he admired physical strength, the dexterity and poise of older boys, the apparently unshakable self-confidence of adult men; soon he sought abrasive comradeship in place of tepid milk tenderness; here too he found himself alone. Conflicts with his schoolmates thrust him into an isolation he soon came to regard as natural and generally valid. While outwardly aloof, somewhat evasive and ironically distant, inwardly he wrapped himself in a cocoon. Eruptions sometimes occurred; he had stormy love affairs that ended disappointingly; his wish to get through to the other person, to find fulfillment and appeasement, became the more dictatorial the higher he set his demands—that is, the more he jeopardized their realization.

## Development of a Beautiful Soul

One trauma arose from his mother's premature death, when he was nine. The women of the house squabbled with redoubled zeal over the orphan. They told him that his mother was in heaven and that he would see her again only if he followed Christianity's pious instructions to the letter, so he became fervently devout. Guarantors for his faith were the women who pampered him. Later he tried to persuade himself that putting up resistance against this avalanche of matriarchal possessiveness had made him incapable of tenderness forever. At school in England (he'd had private tutors till then), the first result of a collision with boys of his own age was the customary brutalization. Soon he not only was informed on all sexual matters in a blatantly trite manner but also was a master in quoting trivial, homespun poetry; the wit of those verses struck a sarcastic note that relegated even the most innocent sexual references to the murky realms of the smutty joke. When he learned jokes on the holiest of subjects—Jesus Christ, the Virgin, the Holy Ghost—he suffered a turmoil of conscience, for his ardent childish faith, escalated by an aunt he loved dearly (a kind of theological bluestocking), made the sin of his bawdiness weigh heavily upon him. But he kept it up, so as not to be considered a bigoted prude by the other boys— and thus committed the first ignominious act of treachery in his life. It wasn't the last.

## Love Bade Him Welcome

When the miracle of first love came his way, he had still not quite conquered his scruples. An English cousin—whose name, Kitty, together with the image of his mother, was destined to represent all that was pure, light, and uncontaminable—came to spend a holiday with him. At first he acted the experienced ladies' man with her; the women who kept vigil over him and the blonde child missed no opportunity to remind them that anything sexual must of necessity be sinful. Soon, though, he was prompted to open derision. Yet he found himself hampered in love, incapable of putting his precocious visions of libertinage into practice. Kitty was so different from the lewd slatterns of his jokes. Her blondness set her apart from the raven-black Circassian odalisques his fantasy painted so luridly. She was chaste. She would become his wife, dressed in traditional white, with a bridal wreath; then off to Venice for the honeymoon. He dare not try out his obscene notions on her. They never got any further—to Kitty's chagrin, presumably—than pecking, petting, and a piquant heaving of pelvises.

He could have kicked himself afterward, naturally. But he found solace in a new concept of love: The unfulfillable was the

ideal—a motto one could invert at will: The ideal was the unfulfillable. This left him free to perform his more liberal tricks
on less ideal objects of love. His first taste of copulation, with a
much older woman on one of his journeys back to school,
sobered him all the more rudely—or rather, this second traumatic experience left him ever more boundless in his demands
and ever more convinced of their unfulfillability.

## Thanatos

What followed he later called "the most eccentric epoch of my
adolescence." In reality it was nothing but a period of natural
fermentation of all his proclivities. His childhood faith lay in
tatters: anything smacking of religion filled him with repug-
nance. But he also turned away from those on whose account
he'd betrayed the fervor of his faith. Soon he despised his blond
schoolmates equally for their vulgarity and for their hypocritical
Protestantism. He called all religious impulses atavistic—intellectual herd-instincts. He not only felt isolated but sought solitude. Pleased with himself for roaming alone in Nietzschean
neo-Gothic realms of the soul, coolly undevout but full of the
most absurd romanticism, he naturally enough considered the
thought of suicide.

The epoch with which this phase coincided—the late 1920s
and early 1930s—beautifully suited such moods. It was full of
those tensions that in politics drive some to fanaticism and others to lethargy. Side by side with eschatological despair there
prevailed a most violent chiliastic promise. True, it was founded
in collectivism: people were promised a brand-new era, a golden
realm of peace on earth, even though they'd but recently been
busily skinning each other alive and were about to stoop to ever
more inhuman deeds. This didn't jibe with the lofty opinion
he'd had of himself as a never-to-be-repeated occurrence in the
universe; in fact, it only fortified his sense of uniqueness and an
attendant exquisite sense of being shunned.

## ... And Resurrection

He studied at Oxford in those days. Then the Spanish Civil War brought about a change in the times. Golden dreams for the future gave way to apocalyptic visions. Everybody bent to shoulder the burden of man's destiny, either by displaying individual resistance to this or that temporal tide, or by shuffling behind the flock like a lamb; moral decisions were taken only in the philosophical-political sense. After he'd gotten over his communist phase, he indulged in a dandylike preoccupation with self; relics of moral propriety landed on the garbage heap; he cocked a snoot at the putatively welcome possibility of resolving individual conflict with the either/or choice between Marxism and fascism, and clung instead to a single category: the aesthetic aspect was all that counted. At some point or another he happened on Valéry Larbaud's *Songs of A. O. Barnabooth* and found to his delight that they fitted him like a glove. He too had been born of affluent parents, and he joyously quoted: *"Hélas, je suis trop riche; le mal ne m'est jamais interdit quoique je fasse."*

*Le mal*: That—according to the usual flat-footed and generally accepted view—was sexuality, as well as savored affluence. He would accord himself both.

It was a fashionable life-program. Unhesitatingly he went straight over the stylistic crest, foppishly deporting himself on the diminishing spiritual wave. Barnabooth served as a model for an attitude that offered an out-of-court settlement on the issue of hating the world and yet longing to embrace it. With a whoop of delight he saw himself as cursed to languish in this form, which seemed to have stepped straight from the pages of some ancient fashion magazine; he approached vice with man-of-the-world nonchalance, not getting involved, envying at a safe distance the sour insurrection of proud drinkers who looked imperiously for self-destruction—no paltry oblivion—at the bottom of a bottle. In the light of his affected Nietzscheanism, their approach seemed more masculine—blonder, so to speak—

than the pitiable compromise with oneself that life in this accursed twentieth century constantly demanded. What he did shrug off was politics. For his kind of world-abhorrence there was no solution to be found in Catalonia. He considered his desperation more complete when leveled at his own person.

## Bittersweet Solitude

There was still alive in him the Levantine, dark, vivacious aspect of his heritage. For a while, casual attempts to drink his way to a lonely peak of alcoholism were frustrated by a weak stomach. More important, he was clever enough to know he was indulging a mood—life-sickness, superfluity, world-weariness, and existence-loathing—in order to keep something going that in fact belonged in the opposite camp. True, he'd never tried to write poetry, but that didn't stop him from feeling like a poet. In the stylized pathos of Barnabooth's verses, in their delicious mixture of decadence and Douanier Rousseau naiveté, he found something that suited the disposition of his soul: a hymn of world acceptance that went beyond the usual peepshow about life's tawdriness; a winningly camp way of upgrading the ethical inferiority of the ephemeral, frivolous, and fashionable; an elegant way to glean divine refinement from the trivial. This sort of thing had its parallel in the Dada ideas of Marcel Duchamp; very well, then. One knew that the world was a slough of despond; Huysmans had seen himself faced with the choice of either bidding it adieu in a monastery or putting a pistol to his head, and now a new generation was on the way to hurling the world's garbage in its face, especially its most treasured and most idolized trash—art. He preferred, like Barnabooth, to be among the artful few who plucked gems from unprepossessing trivia with connoisseur fingers. For example, you could glorify a mundane railway train and make it the symbol of a way of life that, paradoxically enough, represented the spirit of the times just as surely as it stood for quite the opposite.

While his fellow students at Oxford were busy expressing

their disdain for the quality of the era with carefully shabby clothes and hurrying off to Spain to get a coffeehouse view of the dress rehearsal for the Second World War, he decked himself out with the splendor of a Robert de Montesquiou, masqueraded as a Bluebeard with a number of more or less purchased ladies, and tried, when he went on holiday via Paris to Braila, near the Danube delta, to overlook the fact that lice were making themselves comfortable in the upholstery of the Orient-Express.

## Swan Song

The Paris establishment Sphinx quickly reconciled him to sex. What he failed to realize was that it was also laying the trap he would be caught in. From here on in, he chased women, detested them and adored them simultaneously, spoiled them and consumed them ever more voraciously. Inevitably, he realized they could not give him what he sought. The ultimate union, the blossoming on one another, the melting within one another, the deliverance from self, never came about. He certainly did not curb his sexual sedulity on this account. His lovers were legion. But it was all unenviable—the needs of those who had trouble making physical contact with the opposite sex were trifling in comparison with his bitterness in realizing that physical oneness was fate's scornful way of making the sheer illusoriness of psychic fusion painfully clear.

He feasted on this bitterness. He allowed himself to be driven by it, a spiritual refugee, a youthful Ahasuerus. The fact that he was obliged to traverse a whole continent to go to school seemed to symbolize his entire existence. He got heady on verses like:

> J'ai des souvenirs de villes, comme on a des souvenirs
> d'amours.
> A quoi bon en parler? Il m'arrive parfois,
> La nuit, de rêver, que je suis là, ou bien là,
> Et au matin je m'éveille avec un désir de voyage. . . .

Four times a year he went straight across Europe from Braila to London (pausing in Paris) and from London back to Braila (pausing likewise), with the vaulted feeling of accomplishing a poetic act, wherein the man-of-the-world's bittersweet renunciation of solace from the intangible realm of metaphysics found expression, inherently comforting for the simple reason of having been expressed. One day he too would sing:

> *Mon Dieu, il faut mourir!*
> *Il faudra suivre à travers la maladie et dans la mort*
> *Ce corps que l'on n'avait connu que dans le péché et dans*
>   *la joie;*
> *O vitrines des magasins de grandes voies des capitales,*
> *Un jour vous ne refléterez plus le visage de ce passant. . . .*

And one day—or so it seemed then—he would take leave of this existence, like a voyager flitting by as in a mirror, a shadowy being passing through cities, experiences, and people; he would shrug his shoulders and move on. . . .

Of course this was ludicrous, permissible only as a folly of youth. Today, at sixty-five, he was dripping with sweat in an impersonal hotel room in a surrealistic city that irritated him because it was disintegrating, and the memory was part of the past, displaced to another element and frozen in its own reflection. And he was standing there clutching a brochure whose pictures tried to suggest the possibility of a rebirth of this past. Today the thought of death had a different import; that epoch of youthful ignorance appeared to him like a sojourn in a garden of life, full of blood-warm present values that were now lost, misplaced, forgotten.


## To the Other Shore

He knew he could hardly sleep at this time of day, but he lowered the blind with a clatter, undressed, showered, and lay down on the bed, naked and sweating in the heat. He'd hoarded whole packets of sleeping pills, and as he opened one now the temptation to make short work of them and himself and swallow them all at once shot dangerously and substantially through his mind.

The temptation was accompanied by the sarcastic thought that the idea pursuing him—that he would soon die anyway—might prove mantic in a most banal way. (His Armenian grandmother—clairvoyant, so they said—had prophesied to the very day the deaths of two uncles, an aunt, and a much-loved pug.) What prevented him from carrying out the fatal plan was first the thought of the cheap sensation it would cause in the local press, and second the dreadful inconvenience his body would give the hotel management and personnel. He'd avoided making a fuss for his whole life.

## The Usual Misunderstanding

Linda would have placed this irony, dressed in humanitarian delicacy, in a category she called "cynicism," in spiritual allegiance to her feuilletonist friends. In the past she, the American Jewess (this thought came to him with a certain irony too), had often vituperated about this, hinting that it was rooted in his amoral "Levantine" character. There was no denying that she hated him for this quality—and with the same conjugal hatred with which he hated her, intermingled with a kind of embittered affection, a sense of animal relatedness such as yoked cart-horses develop over time. They hated each other in a stereotypical marital fashion; precisely because there was a remnant of warmheartedness clinging to the shackles of habit, each wished the other all the more grimly to hell while simultaneously placing implicit faith in their common devotion.

Still, he would have liked to know how Linda would react to news of his death. Surprised that it hurt, perhaps? But for all her relief, would she detect in her pain and palpable loss a trace of what was known as love?—always bearing in mind the mutations that an initially sentimental, libidinous relationship suffers in the course of a twenty-year marriage. He'd been mulling over this question for years; to put it to Linda straight would have been tasteless, absurd, superfluous. There was no need to discuss such things with women. They disclosed their feelings with incomparably greater honesty in bed than they could in even the most candid conversations. Language, he reflected, contains in each individual word the seed of mendacity; especially in the streamlined tattle favored in fashionable society and issuing from the mouth of a Jewish princess like his wife. How much semantic substance *was* there in the daily chitchat of a chic Manhattanite? Let alone in that of a complex-ridden, blonde, long-limbed, snub-nosed, college-educated daughter of a good Jewish family who had quickly risen to riches and refinement in the best part of tennis-playing Long Island, a lady who would soon have the best years of her life (wasted on him) behind her? Pristine truth in such cases existed only in the matrimonial bedroom.

## Always See the Other Side As Well

He got up from the bed to fetch a glass of water for his pills. Naked, he passed in front of the mirror in the baroque frame— stylistically appropriate to the image of a nude, solidly built man of sixty-five that now surfaced there; not exactly a potbellied, juiced-up Silenus, but still a heavy gentleman one could best imagine as a river god besieged by nubile nymphs perched on a Roman fountain. He was equally plausible as a choice victim for the old man with the scythe, a bony hand holding a hood over the half-hidden, shiny skull. It was hard to imagine this body arousing desire in any woman, and that made Linda's coldness plausible; after all, she clung to the cult of eternal youth as tenaciously as an aging pederast.

How patient he was with Linda! Come to think of it, everything she did got on his nerves, from her morning exercises to her tennis mania to her pretense of smart professionalism and the fuss she made about antinuclear associations and Amnesty

International. It was all so damn fashionable. He bit his tongue to stop from yelling when she discussed macrobiotics, conservation, Zen, even the Filipino technique of bloodless operations, with her friends—artists and journalists who demanded more and more of her time, interests, and purse.

## Language Barrier

Linda spoke a language whose words seemed at first to be related to his and her mutual tongue, but when strung together produced a meaning that sounded to him—on those rare occasions when he got the gist—like a sort of erudite gibberish. Many others admired her for it and encouraged him to join their chant of praise. But he had always thought Linda prosaic, bogged down in platitudes and mediocrity, and he was bowing to the recognition that she was becoming the paragon of all that was unattainable for him, the embodiment of everything illusory and unreal—similar to this city, damned to reflect its own mirage, an eternal incitement to self-deception. In a word: *woman*. It filled his playbill to perfection that *she* was the bearer of original sin.

Perhaps this was why he put up with her, beaten to a docile, unresisting standstill as he was: as though this were his natural birthright as a man, which it was hopeless to oppose. That made his flight ridiculous, the provisional end of his escapade in Venice symbolic. His precipitate departure, with no explanation and no declaration of reason, destination, or duration of absence; his seemingly so arbitrary decision to board a plane in New York and take off in an unknown direction—these might be embarrassing for a man of his caliber; but not really, when one considered he'd been living against his better conscience these twenty years—more like *fifty!*—half a century!—grimly convinced that there was no other curative way open to him, no fundamentally different condition from this equivocal, false-bottomed one between love and hatred. . . .

## Sleep, the Healer

The water dribbling from the faucet of the bathroom sink was lukewarm. Reluctantly he took a sip to wash down a couple of pills and resisted the renewed and now more earnest temptation to swallow the rest he'd spilled on his palm. He decided not to replace them in the bottle but carried them together with a half-filled glass of water to the nickel, glass, and fake-wood night table next to the bed. The room was airless. He lay down, closed his eyes, and waited for the pills to take effect.

The effect never came. Instead the old and familiar experience repeated itself, as so often confirmed in the course of this journey, that the horizontal position is not conducive to inner peace but brings all one's murkiest spiritual dregs to the surface.

Since early childhood he'd gone to bed with the same inner longing for embryonic protection, warmth, and oblivion that had drawn him into women's laps. And just as he'd failed to find what he sought with women and was thrown back with escalating needs and gathering wrath on his own resources, so too, more and more regularly, the desired requital failed to occur in bed. In its place only the discomfort of a heightened consciousness of the world's misery.

This sensation became most violent when both elements—women and bed—combined to parade before him everything that was ugly, obsessed by desire, driven by delusion, yet also unspeakably vulnerable about the wormlike nakedness of his soul and body. Standing on his two legs, armed with the determination of a hunter, brandishing tomahawk or Colt, *Wall Street Journal* or pocket calculator, a man gave off a semblance at least of the myth of *Homo sapiens* as master of the earth (which not even children believed anymore, although the megalomania of technology now claimed to have extended the mastery of the species out into the cosmos), a myth to give him and his fellow men the self-confidence they needed in their roles as studs. But as he lay there helpless, naked and kicking like a baby, his hair

now vestigial to match, the biological truth was starkly revealed: He was a creature inadequately equipped by nature for
the struggle to survive, at the mercy of every injustice, crazed
by fear and therefore ready to resort to any possible means of
self-defense. He was a freak, a hybrid excrescence on the family
tree of evolution, certainly not its crowning glory, although
perhaps its final stage. . . .

## God's Image

. . . and this creature hustled and swarmed and burrowed and
built and destroyed and multiplied and ran wild and spilled
across the planet a kind of mange that stripped it bare and made
it fester—who could not feel desperate about it? During those
first stormy years, when he was young and plucky—fitted out
(if only physiologically) with confidence in life, carried, perhaps, by the remains of his childish trust in God, and soaring in
the clouds of his self-appointed role as a dandy—he'd confined
himself to a select circle of personal, frivolous, egotistical interests. He had had as his credo the idea of going his own way,
teeth firmly clenched, eyes shut tight to avoid noticing the despised, unwelcome aspects of life, on no account enlarging the
field of his engagement beyond the immediate and necessary.
The Lord above, who fed the fowls of the air and clothed the
lilies of the field, could be entrusted with the management of the
enterprise as a whole. He, for his part, wanted to remain in the
most private sector and try to live as hedonistically as possible.

He was assisted in this not only by the epoch itself, in which
such an attitude was still part of a generally accepted scheme of
things (although rapidly becoming suspect), but also by his
inherent (Levantine) cleverness in managing himself. Even as he
eulogized, Larbaud fashion, the morbid delights of the Old
World and partook of what remained of them, he laid plans to
evacuate and head for the New. With nary a pang he departed
from Europe, which was already trading in its identity for a tidy

chunk of America. A considerable fortune had come to him after his father's untimely death, and he made a great deal more money. He made it on his own, not in the abstract void of finance but by applying himself personally and untiringly to a number of growing businesses, in the tradition of his Levantine forebears. Thus did he manage to fill in much of the emptiness yawning in him; for the rest, he performed what he called his "biological mandate."

## Poking Fun at God's Creation

When in the mood for baiting Linda's intellectual cronies, "biological mandate" was how he referred to the happy circumstance he had to thank the war for—which was putting it cynically, to be sure. Confronted with their quickly dying conversation, their covertly exchanged looks of shared loathing, and their not even bothering to object, he proceeded to expound his philosophy with malicious delight, adding insult to injury by scandalously maintaining that wars took place for no other purpose than to remind mankind of this its rightful vocation.

He experienced the catastrophes of his generation from a safe distance, true, but certainly he knew what bloody madness had transpired. At one decisive point the opportunity was accorded him to find out in what horrendous manner the war accelerated not only technological development but also a complete social reshuffle (and with it a complete collapse of conventional order)—a precipitate form of progress which, even before the atom bomb and subsequent unrest around the globe, unleashed unexpected complications and set up a cry for a quick, simplifying, and final solution. Something more than chest-thumping Yankee optimism was called for if one was to avoid concluding that humanity was voluntarily and intentionally working toward the destruction of itself and the whole planet. This was not a new departure; it was cosmobiologically predetermined from the outset.

42

Stars too, he was wont to say, must be included in the divine game of rise and fall. The task of eradicating the globe had fallen to the species *Homo faber*. Hand in hand with the delugelike reproduction of the species went the invention of extermination devices that would wreak abnormally great havoc, making them suitable for helping this planet in the solar system to a "natural" death in the broadest sense of the word. Apart from a handful of geniuses who had long since had foreknowledge of all this and had pitched in to help the destruction along, the great mass of individuals (more than five billion already, isn't that so?) continued to vegetate in the biological dark, vaguely realizing that their part in this game was simply to procreate as many new mass particles as possible. Good humans did this obediently and unflaggingly, while the chosen servants of divine providence worked on the adequacy of the extermination devices. And he too, he told his chilled and silent listeners, piously participated, humbly doing his tiny best to help the universal effort along.

## No Sleepwalking Allowed

The reticence of Linda's friends after such expositions allowed him to slip away to another room to watch television. What he heard and saw there usually fitted the mood he'd left behind.

Fact was, he was convinced of the basic truth of his argument; he really *did* see no other point to the multitude of humanity than life itself, the procreation of a life ceaselessly devoted to dying. His secret grief—that despite all his most extensive efforts he himself had remained childless—was of little consequence. In the industries he controlled, he was often heard to say, achieving a high production quota was often less important than keeping the assembly line rolling.

But he availed himself of such highfalutin metaphors only when *standing*, protected by the armor of his charcoal-gray double-breasted suit. Lying naked, like a gargantuan baby, he was defenseless against the naked facts of the case: namely, that

43

when he performed the act of sexual intercourse, as he did with the passion of an addict, he did so bitterly, driving himself even deeper into a void. Unhappily, it was the passion of a heathen religious fanatic who recognizes the idol he worships as a pale arrangement of wood, wire, leather, and feathers smeared with sacrificial blood but nevertheless falls on his knees and begs for mercy. The act of consecration he strove for whenever he took a woman in his arms, the penitent's journey into extinction of self he embarked upon—each time he had the acute sense that a swindle was about to unfold, a primeval existential lie. Even in the moments when love deluded him into believing it was possible spiritually to merge with the Other and together to pass into the sublime, to evaporate into Being with no beginning and no end—even then, in the fleeting purple ecstasy, he knew he was pursuing a fabled unicorn.

## What It's About

The sleeping pills had no effect, and the dripping bathroom faucet, which he'd neglected to turn off properly, irritated him to the point of making him itch and tremble. He imagined he was swimming, or sitting on mud surrounded by water, with no firm bottom beneath. He hated Venice. It enraged him to think he was damned to wallow here in the smelly slime of the lagoons, dwelling for the umpteenth time on the very same old insoluble crap he'd been at pains to escape during the past four weeks of traveling, waterlogged in the same old bog of inadequacies, swimming against the tide of his complexes, which were nothing but ordinary, dime-a-dozen neuroses anyway.

What on earth was this spook, this shadow play in the inner sanctum of self, this carnival of pictures and words, interplay of both, of obligatory and spontaneous vision, of enlightenment and deceptive deduction? What on earth went on in the illusory hellzapoppin that the emotion-crazed human intelligence staged in collision with reality and that had come to be known as the unconscious? What biological function was fulfilled by its insane delusions, detached from truth and always misinterpreting or quarreling with it? Did humanity derive from this loony circus, this kaleidoscope of random splinters into which perception shattered the world and which it then, eternally and futilely questing for law and order, regrouped into some other partial, fragmentary form? It all revolved around a mere handful of the most primitive elements of existence.

## What It Boils Down to

Here, at the end of the twentieth century of the Christian era after a history of fifty millennia following an evolutionary process that had taken many millions of years, here lay an example of this strange species, naked as his ancestors had been in the loam landscape of China or the East African savannah; lay on a bed in the honeycomb masonry of a Venetian luxury hotel, surrounded by technical gadgets to implement "facility of communications," as Goethe had warned nearly two centuries before; lay there reflecting on a life that had embraced various experiences and given him a more accurate picture of the world's condition than had been accorded most of his contemporaries, despite—or because of—the manically proliferating information media; lay there sweating and mildly dazed by the influence of powerful soporifics, which his metabolism had quickly and indifferently integrated, as it had done with so many previous poisons; lay there brooding about . . . about . . . about what? about the human proscription to loneliness . . . about the decline into oblivion of that which alone could remove the curse: *love*.

## Ye Olde Game

He thought of the thousands of miles of papyrus thickets that had been cut and the legions of yearling kids that had been slaughtered for parchment, the whispering forests that had been lopped down and converted into paper, the hundreds of thousands of barrels of ink and tons of printer's blacking that had been sacrificed to the treatment of this theme, the millions of miles of film on which its images had been imposed, the generations of poets, philosophers, scientists, not to mention novelists, who had consecrated their lives and works to it. Each individual who was stricken by this delirium, tortured (as he'd been till now) by loneliness or, even worse, the fear of it, was also afflicted by a mirage, imagining a possible solution to the dread, and played out the age-old game through all its deadly phases from beginning to bitter end; and was then stunned, felt helplessly abandoned, cruelly exposed, as though he were the very first to suffer the slings and arrows of sex, above all love, as though its delights and disappointments, gaiety and grief had never before existed. . . .

## But There Are Differences

The men out there at the pool with their sunburned, bottle-blonde, gold-glistening women had resigned themselves in a more masculine way to the truth that these conflicts were eternal and the sweet delusions only fleeting. Still, he supposed, they too had not yet grasped how hopeless it was to try to force a realization of love in bed.

Almost everyone had experienced—without learning from it—that in bed love expressed its illusory nature mercilessly. He knew this better than most, from both his marriages. In both he had experienced the disappointment of metaphysical expectations and the rapid ebb of feelings, his own or his wife's. Only the forms in which this was manifested differed, since the temperaments of the two ladies differed. Birgitt, the first, tried quickly to refuse him, with brusque Scandinavian directness. Linda, his present spouse, preferred to take the wind from his sexual sails by allowing him access with total, gum-chewing indifference. In both cases he succeeded in avoiding the cata-strophic mistake of revealing his humiliation, thanks to the im-peccable functioning of his gonads: he resolved to tame his bucking blondes by copulating with each of them constantly, almost blindly, with a regularity they might have thought bes-tially primitive, so much so that they couldn't hope their psy-chological strategies would have any effect. They must have realized how futile it was to hope that resistance or apathy would persuade him of their disappointment.

## Be Faithful to Your Goals

He continued to behave as if he were under love's sweet spell. (In the beginning, ardor had in fact been experienced during the initial exchange of intimacies; with the subsiding of erotic ten-sion it had evaporated, however, to be replaced by a bitter reproach asking that the extinguished feelings be rekindled.) And if he had not only gone on coupling with his no longer loving lovers, imperturbably persistent as before, but also draped them with furs and jewelry and other generous proof of his abundant devotion, this all had happened with a kind of sardonic indulgence, for in the meantime he hated them as surely as he'd once yearned to love them. All the more reason not to admit defeat.

With Birgitt it had been simple. Although she tried to fob him off with cheap excuses, he simply mounted her while she slept—even after he realized that her outrage at this indignity led her to betray him left and right. She began to perform these acts of vengeance with a rabbitlike, nymphomaniacal haste, and eventually came to her senses and turned to him for help. At that point he was readily magnanimous and understanding; he paid her off with a princely sum and, once the divorce was final, set about behaving as though he never wasted another thought on her again.

With Linda things were rather more complex. News of her

sudden death, for example—for all the grateful relief such a smooth and effortless solution would afford to a problem as nasty as an ingrown toenail—might also bring a stabbing pain to his heart; this would betray a shadow of that feeling commonly known as love, although in his case it was a sort of changeling stepchild, begotten of rage and deformed by the impotence of constant repression.

This bastard feeling was lodged in his gallbladder, not his heart. Characteristically, his rancor was directed against his own bondage to the subject of his perverse devotion. Despite all the changes Linda's image had undergone in his mind with the passage of time, and despite the fact that he now found her disagreeable, still he felt bound to her in some mysteriously sentimental way. And this, he knew full well, was why he'd wind up the loser—unless he could think of a solution that was as elegant and definitive as the factual death of one or the other of them.

## Be Polite

The pills on the designer fake-wood night table held promise of the most effective and definitive solution, no doubt of that. His cynicism told him it would be more polite this time not to let his wife precede him through the doorway—even fundamental chivalric duties are subject to modification when circumstances require it. He considered whether or not he should set forth the real reason for his decision in a farewell letter; it would be hard to pin down, of course. Certainly the *misère* of his second marriage was a big factor, but mostly it was the boredom, the fact that for years now his thoughts had been circling fruitlessly around this murky misery, and with an ever more paralyzing sense of futility.

Yet the boredom and misery weren't the only reasons for his condition—the physical hypertension, steaming to all his nerve ends and through all his blood vessels, into the most minute

48

tributaries of his veins, and making him vibrate to his very fingertips, sizzling with resistance to the circumstances of his life. There were all sorts of other reasons, to say nothing of the general state of the world and the incredibly painful and complicated dental work he'd had recently. Yes, there were a host of other reasons for his neurosis, but he didn't care to begin to list them. At the center of these—as Linda's pulp journalists would be bound to say—he himself must be viewed as the prime mover of his self-disembodiment, although in a quite different manner from what they might suspect. His unhappy marriage was a symptom of his condition, not its cause.

## What Is Happiness, Anyway?

Was his marriage in fact so very unhappy? Linda would be astonished and deeply hurt to hear it. In public they passed for a contentedly settled couple; people envied them their dependable good humor and the elegant figure they cut together, admired the warmth with which they greeted each other's friends—even when they hated these cordially and knew themselves to be hated by them with equal intensity. The insidious hatred, the classical matrimonial testiness, and the occasional desire—impossible to avoid and difficult to conceal in any marriage—cheerfully to wring one's partner's neck were not so evident with them as with most other couples they knew (those, that is, who had not yet attained the stage of absolute reciprocal indifference). They gave almost nothing away by chance in their gestures or conversation, and so it came about that their marriage was regarded as more or less a "success," just as everything in his life was bound to turn out "successful."

The unhappiness of this marriage—or what he deemed unhappiness—appeared as inevitable a part of his life as growing old. But something else about it ate away at him, made it the focal point of his existential discontent.

49

## The Spring of Yesteryear

In the beginning, after a rather brief amorous flowering of which he recalled but a few tender moments (fewer than from the period with Birgitt anyway, but of course he was older when he married Linda), in the beginning he had been irritated by her listlessness in bed, particularly since it had set in right after a phase of extreme receptiveness to his sexual favors. He'd been alert enough to recognize soon enough what was happening, and it didn't catch him unawares. Linda withdrew from him in other ways: once she had told him uninhibitedly about the few sexual experiences she'd had before they met; now she became taciturn, and confined herself to the observation that *malheureusement* it had always been thus—a man's erotic attraction wore off after only a brief interval—but it had nothing to do with diminishing affection for him, nor did she regard the physical contact as unpleasant or burdensome; no, it was simply that she no longer could have an orgasm, that was all. Those versed in psychoanalysis were familiar with the phenomenon, by the way; no less than Princess Bonaparte had entrusted herself to Sigmund Freud for this very reason. . . .

It seemed reasonable to suppose that Linda had a secret lover. Pretending to accept the change with philosophical composure, acting in fact as if nothing struck him as odd about it, he began to watch her closely. He even had her shadowed for a while by a private eye—this was admittedly disgraceful—with no result, as might be expected. She worked hard at her undemanding job as public-relations director for a chic publisher of coffee-table books; worried together with her pulp-journalist friends over atomic armament and atomic disarmament, cancer research, and similar human affairs; played an ambitious game of tennis; wove zealously at an extensive network of social obligations, which gave her a pretext to avoid the emotionally charged trial of being alone with him; and then, at lights-out, when he took her in his arms, delicately suppressed a yawn.

## Serious Menace

As was to be expected, his stubbornly persistent copulation campaign proved no match for her in the long run. He could well imagine what would happen if it were to collapse altogether. Even at fifty-five he had had to be fiercely on guard against the idea that he might simply have failed Linda as a man; on no account must he let it unnerve him now, at sixty-five, or he might end up feeling guilty—in the manner of those perennially adolescent gentlemen whose self-respect depends on the quality and duration of their physical prowess. And that was doubly foolish if one was unwilling to concede that the same might be demanded of women, no?

Be that as it may. Among the truths that crystallized in the matrimonial bedroom was the disquieting one that he was no longer half so vigorous as his strategy of undeviating coition demanded. Even when he closed his eyes in order not to see that slight distension of the mouth with which Linda suppressed a yawn, he could hear the deepened intake of breath, and he interpreted her violent expulsion of air afterward not as passion but as quelled impatience; the consequence of such observations, or imaginings, was immediate and difficult to conceal.

## Ex Orienten Lux

Thanks to his blessed Oriental ancestors' fecundity, his gonads, at least, still rallied valiantly. Afterward, however, lying silently on his back once again, he would sense his wife, mute and motionless beside him, and the fury he felt toward her and her corpselike impassivity were not intense enough to repress the realization that when all was said and done she was probably unhappier than he. He could not help feeling traces of guilt, even though they related more to physical than to spiritual matters. Soon he began to ascribe Linda's frigidity to the decline of his sex appeal; and so the idea had wormed its way into and begun to gnaw at his vitals—was it really nearly two decades now?

Time flew by with such lightning speed, it seemed, after a certain age. . . . At any rate he must prevent these guilt feelings from accelerating the process of aging. To put it a different way: He must stop the vicious circle of diminishing self-confidence and actual waning of manliness. (Such processes were known as "escalation" these days; applied visually to this particular syndrome, that term seemed cruelly mocking.)

To be honest with himself—which he wasn't always, any more than being honest with others—he couldn't deny that this condition had already come about. Without certain aids, he wouldn't have been capable of carrying on the campaign.

## But the Play Goes On

After Linda's coldness toward him in bed became apparent and after he determined not to let himself be thrust too far into the background, he began to indulge in so-called "little dabbles on the side." A dated expression, true, but he knew of no better one for the poignantly pinched quality of such deviations from the straight and narrow marital path. This was by no means a triumphant comeback to the libertine glories of yore; he hardly enjoyed these at all. Each new woman served merely to confirm the unimpaired quality of his manliness. He undertook his little dabbles methodically and coldly, so that they were nothing more than rigidly exercised physical jerks. His soul, he said to himself between grimly clenched teeth, belonged to Linda alone.

Although of course both the variety and the fascination of picking up ever new playmates stimulated his sensuality (he treated himself to soberly purchased call girls only when pressed for time, between two flights, for instance, or as a kind of sleeping pill), a complication nevertheless developed. He was not always attracted enough to them physically to forget, in his pleasure, the original purpose. Instead of freeing himself from

Linda in other women's arms, he found himself ever more en-
tangled in thoughts of her. He would catch himself taking out
on another woman the anger he felt toward his own. Or enliv-
ening his erotic fantasies by imagining it was Linda lying there
beneath him instead of the other woman, experiencing—and
demonstrating!—the other's joy. Later, in the reverse situation,
when he came home and fell upon Linda with all this fresh in
mind, it did indeed help him to carry out his program of tireless
fulfillment of his marital duties, despite the absence of tenderness, or least sign of desire, on Linda's part. But no sooner had
he summoned his fantasy to the rescue than it too began playing
tricks on him.

## Vortex

It was but a single—indeed almost unavoidable—step once again
to the treacherous notion that Linda might be as frisky in other
men's arms as those other women were in his. He had no desire
to venture into that kind of bog, especially since now and then
he used precisely this fantasy when he failed to rise to the desired
heights with one of his ersatz partners, or even with Linda
herself.

The resistance he showed to these caprices of his tortured
psyche, despite their intermittent usefulness, was unfortunately
somewhat flaccid. Stiff enough, however, to keep him from
being carried away, from succumbing to the prurient longing to
imagine Linda covered by another man or actually to witness it;
stiff enough to keep him from suggesting this scandalous longing to her.

His reservations were far from prudish. Group sex and wife-
swapping and the like were the middle-class games of today and
were, according to some psychologists, even of therapeutic
value; there was no need to defer to prejudices in this connection
(least of all of class), except those of taste. What gave him
pause—apart from primitive jealousy, which of course flared

within him—was a certain standard of moral hygiene that dictated that erotic discipline and exclusiveness were as indispensable as obeying the prohibition against relieving oneself in public.

Maybe he was holding up his hands in front of eyes that wished to see. There was no longer any need of a chink in the curtain to disclose what lay beyond everything uncouth that civilization had over the course of millennia painstakingly eliminated from man, and also everything it had invested him with and then found wanting and quickly hidden. It wasn't only the animal in us, whose domestication kept the churches so fervently occupied, but also the appalling results of the misguided moral education we had to thank these institutions for: the revolting spiritual homunculus who danced like a genie in a bottle even when he was submerged in the profoundest depths of the soul.

## Beware the Jabberwock

He hated all forms of psychology that took this as their theme. It seemed absurd to the point of insanity to call it the attainment of a high level of civilization when one retrieved this evil-smelling bottle-spirit from the deep by means of supposedly scientific procedures and commanded it to perform in public. For his part he intended to abide by the conventional rules—so far as these were bearable.

He'd always believed that Orientals were incapable of excessive perversion. An Oriental might become addicted to militant sadism, say, or sodomy, perhaps even coprophilia (and even turn it into a religious cult), but never to the cloying erotic antics that even an average Westerner seemed to need to rouse his dwindling sexuality. Until now it had made him proud to think that he, as a half-Armenian (in his freer moments he considered himself a whole one), stood in a more direct and healthy relationship to sensuality than did his other, more lymphatic half, the puritanically austere, covertly and lewdly giggling Englishman who inclined to masochism and worse. So it wasn't prudery when he put a stop to certain erotic (eroticizing!) imaginings. A psychiatrist would surely seize on these fantasies and use them in service of the only goal that seemed dear to the hearts of these shamans of the Freudian credo: proving anew the accuracy of their sacred texts. He could happily dispense with such corroborations. Greenhorn layman that he was, he could advance his self-analysis unaided to those strata where a few mythlike banalities are models for all forms of spiritual inhibition. And so he saw the capricious fantasies with which he tried to transform the autumn of his virility into a blooming Indian summer as ribaldries that Linda drove him to indulge in against his inherently chaste nature. And this insight more or less canceled out the insidious guilt feelings he harbored about her.

He sometimes dwelled on this in genuine outrage, which helped him to a further simple but appalling insight: the natural symptoms of aging had been worsened by the sublime castration perpetrated on him by his wife.

## Subtleties

Would it be tactful to mention this to Linda in his farewell letter? To whom else could he address it, if not her? He had no friend he might talk such things over with—had never had a really intimate friend, in fact, only herds of supposedly amicable business and social acquaintances (who could have been exchanged for those lying around the pool without anyone's noticing the switch), and he knew they were waiting to detect weakness in him. What a cackling and crowing there would be if they heard that the cause of his suicide was the hoary old platitude about flagging erotic appeal in a twenty-year marriage. Even in ephemeral liaisons, less strenuous if only because of less time spent together, a certain weariness was bound to set in; this was as reasonable to expect as "Amen" at the end of the Lord's Prayer. With an erotic past as colorful as a peacock's tail, he should have known this better than anyone. And although it was irritating that actually it had been Linda and not he who early on had shown the first sign of this inevitable development, he should have been grateful for the pretext she gave him to think about the identical course of his extramarital but, as it were, legitimized relationships.

## Don't Forget the Whip

There was no denying that his attitude was laughable, trivial. His refusal to accept things as they were was ludicrous, a boyish defiance foolishly prolonged into old age, evidence of provincial narrow-mindedness and bad taste, not to mention several graver flaws of character. It was obvious, for instance, that the Oriental in him still fondly nurtured the concept of woman as sexual slave. Anyway, Linda was bound to think this, and it probably strengthened her inner resistance to him.

Still, he was convinced, in principle, of the tactical and ethical soundness of his position. It might look like a brusque demonstration of asinine machismo, but it could just as well be interpreted as the hallmark of gentle chivalry. Was it not the most beautiful compliment a woman could receive, when a man professed—and proved!—to love and desire her quite as much after twenty years of marriage as he had on their first night? Besides, although this was a personal matter, it did have a general, fundamental dimension: the shared agony of their inability to unite had insidiously become visible. A devilish perfidy ensured that isolation was at its worst precisely when two individuals were at pains to become *one* flesh and *one* spirit: *in the sacrament of marriage!* . . . Laying down your weapons in marriage was tantamount to unconditional surrender to the enemies of love.

## Inevitable Self-Mockery

How amazed his various so-called friends (above all those who posed as intimates but wished him humiliation, first and foremost Linda's pulp journalists), how surprised that company of ill-wishing contemporaries would be when they discovered he could become positively religious by contemplating a mundane sexual calamity. He felt his facial muscles twitching. They'd glimpsed only the most superficial of his spiritual dimensions; there were others, of an other-guess kind, that would flabbergast them even more.

Be that as it may. Let the matter rest. His present condition resulted from an unfortunate series of interrelated circumstances, and he couldn't change them as he was used to doing in other fields. That was all. In light of the myth that he, like everyone else, had built around his own person, he must never betray the inner laceration. It was a matter of professional conscientiousness. The image was of a man who calmly pulled life's strings; it must not be distorted into that of a problem-ridden neurotic brooding on the meaning of life.

But of course, again like everyone else, he carried another secret, tenderly cherished image of himself. In it he enjoyed incomparably greater freedom of thought and emotion, could dream of being a much more complex person, a person to whom power never meant anything. Power was merely a necessary article, a side effect that appeared whenever certain elements of the game—notably money—achieved extraordinary proportions. If he had indeed shown great skill in this game, it had to do with his calm and prudence, an ability to act quickly and instinctively, as well as a despotic detachment, not natural to him but the result of iron self-discipline. He was a poet at heart, he knew. If his imperturbability seemed like coldness, lack of consideration for others—well, the reasons for this were commercial not personal. *Voilà,* the cobbler's thumbs: *déformation professionelle.* He bowed to the logic of what he was dealing with—money. The persona of a cast-iron financier was superimposed on his real self like a crust of ice over a geyser; beneath the ice there bubbled a warmer self that at times erupted; he'd held the eruptions in check until recently, until this last one, which had driven him to Venice.

## Escape Banality with Banalities

It was typical of the design of his destiny that things appeared to be other than what they were, so probably not even Linda noticed a link between this last eruption and his disappearance from New York. Although she knew that he loathed traveling ("After going hundreds of miles back and forth to school, I lost the taste for it"), occasional business trips of some days' or even weeks' duration were not to be avoided. He owed no one an explanation, not even Linda; nor did she expect any, her equable temperament restraining her from such personal, possibly indiscreet interest. She continued to run her household and social life as if her busy husband were expected back tomorrow or the day after at the latest, and wasted no time wondering about the purpose or location of his absence.

For thirty years his secretary too had accustomed herself to accepting the unexpected as customary; he was reticent and spontaneous in his business dealings as well. Of course she would realize it was four weeks since she had heard from him. She knew his patriarchal, Levantine homeliness and his restless energy, the way he normally concerned himself with even the most trifling business details, and she would wonder. But that didn't mean much. For the moment he was simply "out of town." It still wasn't known that this was a dropping out—out of life itself, perhaps.

The sensation caused by an act of emotional disturbance, which his suicide would certainly be and which would posthumously alter his image, was still in the balance. Only when the news had broken would conjecture and perplexity begin. They could never glean, from the telltale splinters of the shattered picture, an inkling of the simple truth. He'd had his fill, as much as he could take, for years; he was frightened not so much of old age and death as of the futility of his existence—of existence, period; a vague guilt clouded his well-being and his common sense like a pea-soup fog. . . . When you came right down to it, this climacteric was typical neither of the money-and-power-and-glory-grubbing troglodyte nor of the camouflaged poet alone, but of everyone who had ever had a leaf from the calendar blown in front of his feet by a gust of temporal wind and had been awakened from the sleepwalk of existence. . . . This was reason and occasion for suicidal desperation.

## Those Bygone Years of Individual Guilt...

The bygone years surfacing now on the current wave of nostalgia—the years of the *grands trains de luxe*, the brand-new Charleston rage, the page-boy hairdo; the roaring twenties and early thirties, times in which he'd exclusively bled his poetic vein (on the Orient-Express and at the Sphinx, principally)— were, in comparison with today, anything but innocent, no more than himself. But his sense of guilt then had been more tangible and personal, had related itself to particular sins and offenses, defined precisely in the moral code of the epoch and of his class. Before he had created his putatively cynical but in reality quite desperate image, when he thought of self-criticism as a characteristic of a higher nature (thanks to the humanistic ideas drummed into him), he had been ashamed of the insolence of his actions and even more of his aptitude for performing all kinds of disgraceful acts, cruel ones too, on other people (usually lovers), as though obliged to do so by his inherent makeup, unfortunately stronger than his moral conviction.

## Collective Self-Contempt...

His older schoolmates had already discovered Freud by this time. He avoided the temptation of burrowing in his past to find out which of his early experiences was responsible for the inferior quality of his superego compared with his shady instincts and proclivities. It was simpler to follow those who ascribed the fragility of his moral nature to his Levantine heritage—even in tolerant old England such racist innuendos were not quashed. It didn't make things any pleasanter, of course. Sometimes—when the thought of his ignoble nature could no longer be vanquished by the dream of the day when his Anglo-Saxon, blond side would triumph at last, like Siegfried emerging from the woods after slaying the dragon—he had genuinely despised himself, however rebelliously, proudly, defiantly. His self-contempt perfectly matched the general world-contempt.

## ... And Individual Angst

Nowadays, quite different guilt gnawed at his inner peace, and it put personal guilt in the shade. He deemed himself conjointly responsible for the collective sin with which humanity as a whole was risking its life—oh, not in the way Linda and her spiritual cohorts blathered on about the shocking materialism and faithlessness of the Western world, about ecology, whole-grain diets, and the like, about the consistent outrage against Mother Nature that would soon peak with the cobalt bomb. No, he was focused on the blinding act of self-repression that so devilishly robbed the world of its poetry; the inability (or unwillingness?) to grasp the enormity of death and, by showing it reverence, to sanctify life; to look on one's fate to destroy and be destroyed as a creative commission, and to celebrate this appalling realization by joining the Maker in hoots of laughter; to build a temple to insanity and to celebrate it there.

## God's Bard

As he was thinking all this, he remembered a gray day in New York into which brass-bright late-autumnal sunshine streamed. He had come from a downtown lunch that had gone on and on. His car, which should have come for him at the unobtrusive but excellent restaurant, had failed to show up, and so he'd gone on foot along Twenty-fourth Street to Madison Avenue to look for a cab. The sunlight glistening over the canyons spilled across the airspace above Madison Square and gilded the skyscrapers around it so that they appeared to be floating. For several minutes, until another sheet of rain doused it, this golden light transfigured the flats of the set that for decades had been the barely noticed backdrop of his daily routine and it became a magical futuristic city of almost celestial beauty. The square, where Madison, Broadway, and Fifth Avenue all converged—and you all know what a flotsam and jetsam of humanity flows along them!—was plastically surrounded by monuments of golden promise. The nightmare turmoil of New York—the declared macabre capital of the sinking Western world—the crazed rush and gush in its abysslike streets, the blindly flailing daily fight for survival all at once had a transcendental point of view, which determined a meaningful perspective. Ultimately the aim of all human attainment was divine service and the quest for God. The tower of Babel was also God's work. New York was a single prodigious temple to Mammon, a foul, fun city of which he was sick and tired, a cloying, hated and loved agglomeration of concrete and glass and steel stalagmites sprouting from cesspools and garbage heaps of humanity—New York harbored a fervor that now, on sight of the beauty suddenly emerging, sent tears rushing to his eyes.

He forgot his taxi. Something within him commanded him to hold and cherish this moment as though it contained the visual essence of the whole present epoch. He walked up Madison Avenue with his head held high, like a gaping country cousin. To his surprise, the mood was similar to what he had felt in his youth, when he'd left Europe to come to America, and the memory of that time crowded back in on him with disturbing actuality. They did indeed have something in common, those late twenties–early thirties and this present. He was far too busy enjoying the reunion to figure out what it was.

## And Yet . . .

Here and now, in his hotel room in Venice, he mobilized even less energy to resolving the question. It was quite simple, really; the commonplace view was the right one: The affinity between

61

the two epochs lay in their particular condition of decay necessary to regeneration, their being in a phase of cultural rotting in which a stormy waste process created a kind of hybrid bacterial energy and with it the youthful feature of reform and revolution; from the most mature area of decomposition, life of a special tropical kind was springing up. That had been all too evident in the Europe of the twenties, when the real discovery of America was made—in the legendary Jazz Age, that is; and now it was unmistakably reblossoming in the slums and bohemian quarters of America's big cities. If it were not for a certain hygienic sterility, one might have had reason to fear that America's ripe soil, with its fertile blacks and imported European compost, might be preparing itself for a development similar to that of Europe in the thirties—Nazism, for instance—only, like everything else in the New World, in gigantically overblown form. Pessimists were already proclaiming as much with the splendid gloom of apocalyptic prophecy.

## And Yet . . .

But it was precisely *that* which made the difference; in the twenties no one had foreseen such apocalyptic consequences. On the contrary: there had reigned a besotted general belief in world regeneration; the times had judged themselves not exactly young but at least capable of rejuvenation. "Youth" began storming toward its apotheosis, and people everywhere strove for curative reforms. Technology developed with breathtaking speed and held promise of a bright future. The beauty he'd seen in the golden towers around Madison Square was but a pale reflection of those earlier visions of future cities, of the *one* city of sunlit heaven-high temple-towers that a new, physically fit, blithely cosmopolitan humanity free of racial prejudice would build itself. . . .

This propitious mirage of things revived from the earlier

period, outshining everything else, gave way to the view (across a derelict continent and the graves of forty million humans killed violently) that the world had been in a state of greater innocence: it had been more compact, so to speak, more genuine, not only in its vital, future-oriented essence but right there in its physical structure. Even its junk, its refuse, seemed more solid than that of today—a fact well known to the antique dealers who supplied Linda and her friends. Bakelite was more thoroughbred than plastic; Art Nouveau and Art Deco had more intrinsic artistic worth than pop or conceptual art—this too was well known to the collectors, who regularly prompted Linda's mother to green envy and purple rage, to fuming that she'd been cheated in the race for the latest priceless thing. Something of substance was now missing, something that had made not only the objects themselves more lucid but also the life with them richer, fuller.

Something fundamental had disappeared from the world that—not only according to legend—all living creatures seemed to have had implicitly in common, even in times of strife; something like a shared belief in its continuance. There was a future that promised betterment, the Kingdom of Rapture here on earth, and all eyes turned optimistically toward it, but it was decisively true that the present contained livelier life; even the threats and tensions that split it apart seemed more stimulating and colorful than anything the future might hold. Life had been more livable when the *grands trains de luxe* chugged through the night flashing their beams of light across continents, dream vehicles for all those who lived in darkness too. (That the visions had been optical illusions and their realization appalling—that was another story.)

He did his best to resist the temptation to glorify this past which had been his youth. Yet he thought back on those days as possessing something ineffably pure, like a bouquet of blossoms in the hands of a young girl.

True, his personal history bore no witness to this. Certainly the dichotomies between brothel-schooled libertinism and vestigial Christian ethics, between dandyism and the amorous ideology of Provençal troubadours could not be reconciled with his world-weariness and his carefully timed fits of self-destruction. They were bursts of rebellion that dwindled into gestures, as with someone who grimly sets about to commit hari-kari but doesn't get to his entrails because he can't decide whether they'll protrude more prettily if he draws the blade from right to left or from left to right—narcissistically observing his hesitations and doubts in the mirror all the while.

All of this was kid stuff—in which, to be sure, much that was characteristic of the time manifested itself, for the zeitgeist was not free of contradiction, and foolish dreams of the future went hand in hand with depressing suspicions that the twenties were but an epilogue. Yet the fever chart of his own maturation could hardly be called typical of the time, for his was a young person's experience as it might have been in any epoch; even today. Common to all eras was the way young men expressed emotions peculiar to that stage of life in which they hurled themselves into being "members of the new generation," only to be baffled, betrayed, sold down the river in a world recklessly mismanaged not only by their fathers but by creation itself. Between the ages of sixteen and twenty-four came the moment for reckoning accounts, but one failed to reckon with the passing of time. According to an old Armenian saying, you noticed you'd grown out of your clothes only when they were too small for you. And so, quite independently, he had flirted with suicide, the feeling of sin and danger deliciously thrilling. . . .

Soon, he told himself, he'd have at his disposal a handful of cogent arguments against a too hasty departure from this world. For instance, one might subvert oneself by being excessively and sensitively aware! Blinded by the flood of enlightenment, one might destroy oneself as effectively as with a drug; surely more courage and defiance were needed to look clarity in the eye than to dope up; the pain gained in this homeopathic way, and the desperation, were sublime; this couldn't be achieved in a termination of life by questionable expedient.

## But We Are Honest

He'd soon grown out of such sophistries. Much more effective was the discovery of a maliciously amusing game that took as its subject exactly what legions of world-reforming foot soldiers had claimed was the prime reason for humanity's desolate condition. He reached out and grabbed the golden calf; cleverly and assiduously, he applied himself to the business of making money.

It once pierced his heart to think there would be no one to leave his millions to, but this cruel cut had long since healed. He'd simply send the dough back where it came from, to the so-called world at large—hospitals, museums, libraries. One of the more poetic aspects of America was the way knaves repeatedly appeared on the scene who spent their lives raking in shekels and then gave them away again at the end. Servants of God. This knavery helped him on the road toward what the New World called establishing one's identity. Those of his qualities which, after screening them for light and dark, he'd sought to suppress could now bloom. It was deeply satisfying to hear himself referred to as monstrous, unfeeling, lacking in consideration, a man who'd stop at nothing. Such a reputation gave him elbow room.

Which he exploited rapaciously. True, his disgust with the cringing servility to which money drove even respected people often boomeranged; yet there was no denying the advantages of affluence. Apart from everything, he could now indulge the luxury he enjoyed most—that of spoiling women, bowing to their caprices, fulfilling their most extravagant wishes. It always pleased him to watch women spending money. But alas, here too times had changed, here too quality had been diluted.

## Special Frustrations

Linda proved inflexible. In the image she created of herself—blonde, long-limbed, well aired, elegant, intelligent—there was also a certain bourgeois pettiness, a kind of Jewish common sense. She cared nothing for jewelry she would have to keep at the bank for safety's sake. She declared that six furs were enough to ensure her high position on the list of New York's best-dressed women. She showed little taste for lavish investment in gowns and dresses; sooner than her contemporaries she realized that sartorial elegance was no longer enough to symbolize social standing and that modish superiority could now be exhibited only in the decoration of one's home. Collecting pictures, especially those of contemporary artists (which her mother did with sharklike energy), left a bitter aftertaste, betraying its social-climbing purpose. What remained was home sweet home, the most intimate realm.

Linda's ambition to triumph in interior decoration discomfited him. He was a man of regular tastes, and it hardly pleased him to see his home turned topsy-turvy every third or fourth year, transported each time into a different period style, filled with different furniture, pictures, carpets, bibelots, cutlery, glasses, bedclothes. But since it was his sole opportunity to indulge Linda's fancy, he suffered it patiently. She replaced his beloved (and valuable) collection of English walnut pieces with a complete set of Louis XIV, very shortly afterward with a heap of Art Deco trappings, which were then thrown out to make room, penitently, for the rosy cherry of the Second Empire and next the delights of the Wiener Werkstätte. He suffered it all, teeth gritted. Meanwhile the Braques and the Gris, with which Linda had deftly juxtaposed some Queen Anne furniture, gave way first to several Impressionists, then to de Kooning, Rothko, Kline, then to Klimt and Schiele. Linda was now busy specializing in the so-called *peintres pompiers* of the École des Beaux-Arts.

Yet he couldn't help admiring her. Once her infallible instinct had prompted her to speculate very profitably in Baisse. She bought the furniture and pictures cheaply, before anyone had time to catch her at it, and then sold them at enormous profit. And so there came about the grotesque situation that he was deprived of his one financial approach, for Linda's hobby now financed itself.

## A Love Nest

Their house in Southampton, to which they fled each weekend to escape the hectic monotony of the Manhattan everyday, was largely spared this addiction to changing backdrops (an abstract form of travel, an expression of a compelling nomadic hankering to transcend space by varying the temporal). Fifteen years earlier, when general opinion had dismissed such a plan as being in bad taste, Linda had filled the place with Early Americana, of which each piece was now worth a small fortune. Strangely enough, claustrophobia attacked him there as never before. In the phony atmosphere of Pilgrim-father coziness, among rough-hewn furniture, homespun rugs, carbines, powder horns, embroidered antimacassars, and quilts, surrounded by touchingly primitive family portraits depicting neither his nor Linda's beloved forebears, and rocking horses and dolls belonging to children they also didn't have, his patience came to an end.

They drove out one Friday evening as usual. The customary packing scene, in which under Linda's supervision an entire household was removed by the Italian chauffeur, the Chinese cook, and the black maid, had frazzled his nerves more than usual. A snarled expressway had done the rest. He arrived in the filthiest of moods, and he refused to take the blame for it. He felt helpless, at Linda's mercy, having to battle against the armada of *things* she pitted against him. For this he would have banished any other person from his life forever, but in Linda's case the imponderabilia of love set in—yes, love.

67

## Side Effects

It was hardly surprising, this persistence in calling such a thing love; God knows, all sorts of things masqueraded under that name. In any event it was grim, and it poisoned his world. Even when something about Linda managed to please him—her elegance in an evening gown, for instance, or the spare, thoroughbred economy of movement as she raised a slender arm to her hair (its artful, twenties-style gamine cut emphasized her youthfulness, especially since she had allowed it to go gray, accentuating the color with silver rinses, of course)—even as a little wave of approval rippled through him, he would simultaneously feel the dammed-up resentment at twenty years of defeat in their marriage bed. A choking hostility to everything feminine would inundate him, paralyzing and shaming. Linda's journalist pals would have been happy to show him how this contradictory behavior had evolved, and he laughed at the thought that if he had been younger and dumber, he might have wound up on a wipable couch. As if one could find the key to the problems of marital life in the dregs of the soul! To begin with, it was all pure chemistry in his case: Linda's physical aversion, aggravated by his insistence on regular sexual intercourse, and then a flagging of the functioning of his glands. Yes, that's what had pushed his misogyny over the top; and if he'd had more than his share of "crises" (in recent decades the word had been applied so often to trivial political and economic events that it was robbed of weight, but in private use it still retained shock value), not only he but hundreds of thousands of others besides suffered this. The sheer banality of his condition disturbed him more than the condition itself.

## Never Take It Personally

The outward signs of these crises were exactly opposite to tumultuous. He might, for instance, fall silent in the middle of a conversation, with a vacant expression, his gaze directed rigidly into space, flickering nervousness perceptible only in his heaving chest, and by this behavior seek to suppress the desire to perform some mad and violent act—to launch his fist at the face of whoever happened to be sitting across from him, say. Or he might suddenly stop, wherever he was, walking or standing, and try to jolt his awareness of having picked up something without knowing why—as at the hall porter's desk when he'd taken the Orient-Express brochure.

For his subconscious to have prompted him to reach for the brochure, as might be argued, seemed a scornful trick for life to play on him. It was true that the cover, with its laughable depiction of the defunct European beau monde boarding a luxury train, had brought something home to him in which he recognized the final and decisive cause of his neurosis. Dogged by the ghost of that epoch, he knew on the one hand that he'd served his time and would soon (whether naturally or by his own doing) abandon the rat race, and on the other that his earthly wanderings were redundant and futile, that he and the whole world had declined into desperate poverty in the short half-century since. Like a hurt finger that one tries to protect but succeeds only in banging the more, his dread of death—and synonymously, the vacuity of his life—arose before him in the very visual symbols he sought to escape.

The painful wound was not his alone. Whenever a mention of the past brought bubbles of cast-off life popping to the surface of the cesspool called memory, splattering him rudely with a forlorn realization of his life's awful void, he was not alone. The zeitgeist made him react thus; he was living in the collective mood of the present era. The current flavor of life was one of irreplaceable loss, of that lost innocence which not only he but the rest of the world too had gambled away.

## Fate Is Personal

Still, what a vast difference between his personal sensitivity and that of the commune! The commune was not mortal: the five-billion-headed hubbub of humanity renewed itself ceaselessly, dedicated every waking moment to its own reproduction. The sum total of those living at present was timeless; whether yesterday merged with today or today with yesterday made no difference. The melancholy yearning for the past was eternal too; nostalgia was a component of every folk song, and the sense of lost innocence was as old as the world.

But he would soon—how terribly soon!—die. The innocence he had lost had been his own, even if his life and times had lost its along with him. He couldn't afford a fashionable resuscitation of the past. It tortured him to actualize the smoky moods from distant, burned-out days—as, for example, when he picked up some object he'd once used that had since fallen into disuse (a set of cutthroat razors he'd inherited from his father, which vividly conjured up his image: a heavy man, as he himself was today, with violet lips beneath the luxurious black moustache, and in his eyes the millennial melancholy of a people doomed to suffering); or when he heard the opening bars of an old popular song, a trite melody in which he'd invested the excitement of his youth; or when he spoke a catchphrase that had otherwise gone under with the years, a word from one of the languages he'd heard spoken all around him as a boy (Romanian, Armenian, Bulgarian, Turkish); or when he caught a scent wafted in from afar (chamomile; the pungent smell of burning potato tendrils and mutton sausages, roasted over an open fire in the field; certain perfumes; the violet and rose waters his Armenian aunts had doted on; the camphorized sandalwood chests where they carefully laid their cashmere shawls and gold-shot muslin) . . .

## Death Is a Verdict

His useless life and proximate death gazed blankly at him from each of these impressions. Each time the dissolving picture of a discarded situation overcame him with the inevitable avalanche of betrayed ideals, dreams, promises, the fear of having to die sprang up at him. There was no hope of reparation. From the vantage point of his own bier, his life from childhood to senility presented itself in ever-solemnizing phases of tarnishing luster, of hardening, of disillusionment, a chain of events that in one way or another, whether invoked by him or by mere force of circumstances, testified against him.

His nostalgia was not painful and sweet like the fashionable kitsch version that today's youth wallowed in; not an opportunity offered by the winds of time to disguise himself; not a sentimental tribute to the eternal past, a dream of a fairy-tale world of lost paradises. His nostalgia was a verdict. In the isolation of dying, what still bound him to the rest of the teeming, unendingly procreating brood of humanity was nothing but guilt, as if his personal offenses had been the cause of the world's present brutalization, as if he alone had gambled away the magic of those distant days.

Perhaps his journey wasn't quite so aimless. It had quite literally taken him right around the world and back to where he began. The spherical form of the earth thwarted his flight from himself. One slipped out the back door only to walk in again by the front. The point of the exercise was to see whether one had gained a world or lost it.

All right, then. His reaching for the Orient-Express brochure was not as accidental. Certainly there'd been a soupçon of malice somewhere. He now remembered that as he picked up the brochure he had thought how much Denise would have loved to travel with him on this train. She had had an insatiable weakness for the kitsch of the big wide world.

## Everlasting Episode

Denise! Denise Kugler! (Pronounce it in the French manner: *Kooglaire.*) A "little dabble" who had proved to be quite a handful. She was the last thing he wanted to think of now, although he'd known all along that she was a key figure in the comedy of his neurosis and in the flight from it to Venice. He wanted to avoid admitting to himself that his affair with her (in its fourth year now!) was as powerful a bond as his marriage with Linda, although in her case irrational love truly played no part; also, his hatred for what he thought of as her vulgarity wasn't special enough to warrant a lasting tie.

With Denise he had performed more readily and more reliably than with any other woman in the past three years. Ridiculous to speak of sexual bondage. It was probably due to her inexhaustible capacity for orgasm, just what he missed in Linda. It was also, presumably, the reason why he hadn't left her after one or two encounters, as he was in the habit of doing with his other dabbles. Of course, there was the matter of what Denise referred to as her "nanny hand"—but he chastely forbade himself to dwell on that just now.

Denise entered his life as an employee of the salon Linda engaged to tend to her beauty care, at a time when she had injured her knee at tennis and was unable to leave the house for weeks on end. He had walked without knocking into the room where Linda was having her treatment. With a single glance he took in the gently rounded figure of the white-smocked ministrant kneading his wife, the platinum Christmas-tree-angel hair, curly as a handful of fresh wood shavings, the starry eyes that the beauteous beautician raised to his, her plump rump and well-formed legs. All these held promise not only of an enjoyable exchange of profligacy but of immediate fulfillment as well.

Linda's leg was in a plaster cast, her face covered by a mask of black mud, and there were little damp cotton pads on her closed eyelids. He asked her something about a party they were supposed to attend, and her answers came in a remote and alien tone, as though issuing from an oracle. The effect was comical, and he exchanged a look and then a wrinkle of amusement with Angel Hair; this instantly established an intimacy between them that seemed like a betrayal of Linda. But it didn't of course prevent him from scribbling on a pad of paper the address of a small bar, tearing off the sheet, and handing it to the younger woman, who quickly took it, smiling triumphantly.

He would have many more occasions to feel ashamed of his relationship with Denise and, most especially, of his attitude toward her, even after he removed her from Linda's immediate field of vision and beyond the precincts of Linda's moral jurisdiction, so to speak, by setting her up in her own salon. She was from Alsace, of German descent, but here in New York she played the part of what she thought an amorously capricious yet modern and "enlightened" Parisienne would be like. This creature had, one might guess, been projected from the glossy pages of French women's magazines, in Denise's fantasy a ratatouille of Françoise Sagan, Coco Chanel, Brigitte Bardot, and Martine Carol. But in reality Denise was a little demoiselle from the French sticks, clothed in cheap boutique clothes and malformed by every banality and mediocrity that the French way of life, love, and Lucullan indulgence had to offer. She herself couldn't have judged the American influence on this ideal, not knowing that in New York, a city that effusively welcomes all forms of banality and mediocrity, there was no chance to rise above the average.

Denise was a passionate, indeed virtually addicted, moviegoer and devourer of women's magazines, and she applied the instruction gleaned from these two sources diligently and separately. The spiritual fodder in *Marie Claire* and *Elle* she found correct and beneficial, whereas her wardrobe, her apartment, in fact her entire life-style were modeled on silver-screen oldies, especially those she found "sexy" and "feminine" (the Myrna Loy–William Powell Thin Man comedies were her favorites).

Thus it was his stomach-churning fate to be received by his mistress in an ankle-length gown buttoned at the throat and with a Pierrot collar cascading around her shoulders, in the "pink salon" of her tiny apartment. The background included phony-rococo furniture, rock-hard silk-covered cushions, the sterile rustle of taped "romantic music," and the ritual of cocktails—an extremely complicated ceremony that he regarded as nothing but an aggravating and time-consuming curtain-raiser.

Despite Denise's intent, the ingestion of several repulsive and unpalatable concoctions, mixed according to some star barman's arcane recipes, and extravagant quantities of salted peanuts and almonds did nothing to improve his mood. And she didn't generate much excitement when she exchanged her more formal gown for a backless, indeed almost bottomless, baby-doll nightie and then admitted him to her bed—an elaborate construction of gathers, smocking, chucks, and cunningly complicated pleats, gay rosettes, billowing frills, and flounces of pearl-gray damask. What then occurred was, however, very much to his taste. It wasn't only that Denise had an enchantingly lovely body and a way of effusively reciprocating his smallest caress; above all he valued her nanny hand, the specialty she had skillfully cultivated as much from relish as from conscientiousness. Its name, she archly declared, was due to its ability to "raise the little one to be a big strong man."

At first he reacted to Denise's resolute, active solicitude with an involuntary and surprisingly intense resistance, only to surrender to it all the more readily later. It took a while for him to realize that her technique owed its perfection not so much to sheer professionalism as to a naive delight in sharing the delight of the partner. Basically it contravened the already rather bedraggled myth of his ever alert masculinity to allow himself to be treated like this. His machismo was challenged; up to now he had been the one to initiate foreplay and determine its subsequent course. Although at first he was repelled by her technical dexterity (motivated by a prudery stemming from memories of the Sphinx, of which he was deeply ashamed), before long he succumbed to it and to her touchingly zealous eagerness and her childlike rapture at success.

No kindred erotic stimulation of her own body could ever bring Denise to a comparable state of ecstatic readiness; each quarter-inch's growth achieved under the expertly tender caresses of her lips and fingertips was greeted with little shrieks of joy, exorbitant praise, and a shower of kisses as she anticipated the titillating things to come when the proud results of her

74

labors would be accommodated elsewhere about her person. Bashfully relieved, he knew that this welcome treatment released him from the necessity of monitoring his virility and his own hysterical reactions to its delay (or no-show).

Denise's caresses were invariably successful. Yet they also held a certain latent danger, which he discovered when, with his self-confidence thus newly reinforced—if not wholly restored—he extended the pattern of his dabbles to include her, that is, cheating now not only on his wife but also on his steady girlfriend. This led to unpleasantness when he forthwith expected the same lovingly comprehensive treatment from his casual partners. Already with Linda he failed to evoke the desired response if, lying on his back in a way that had become habitual, he closed his eyes and folded his hands behind his head and waited to be cosseted. Now not only beyond the boundaries of his "rightful" precincts (Denise's damask tent and his own matrimonial bedroom) but also within them, the innovation resulted more often in vexation than enjoyment.

He could have limited himself to Denise alone as his established (and most accommodating) mistress. Indeed, one look in the mirror should have made the wisdom of such a move clear. He had lately turned very gray and become rather heavy; even his bright mountain-shepherd's eyes would not be troubling women's hearts much longer. He could count the days left until even the thrill of variety would no longer make a nanny hand superfluous, until even its sweet ministrations would have to be so intricate and protracted that he could not expect them of casual partners.

Denise herself seemed to take it for granted that theirs would be a solid and lasting relationship. She had little doubt (especially after he had set her up in her own *salon de beauté*, Chez Denise) that he too meant to confer upon his regular visits to the damask tent some sort of institutional nature. She had been raised a devout Catholic, and she blushingly admitted that even now she continued to go to confession in order to be absolved from something that for her was a mortal sin and for which she would otherwise be punished with the eternal fires of purgatory—adultery. She made no bones about her belief that only a union legitimized before God in a church would later exonerate them from their joint blame.

With a mixture of astonishment and sweet tenderness he observed how this fantasy appeared to awaken in Denise a genuine feeling for him. Undoubtedly the fact that he was a rich and powerful man figured largely, but that didn't bother him; he knew that power was an effective aphrodisiac. Yet the heartfelt attraction she displayed for him was clearly called forth by the vision of a shared future, which in her rose-colored mind resembled the fading of a bright summer's day into a long, tranquil evening.

He could not bring himself to tell her how illusory this picture was. Touched and irritated at once—and also curious, scientifically interested, so to speak, in the physiology of the birth and death of human emotions—he let things take their course. Denise soon showed evidence of contented domesticity in a variety of ways. She expanded the cocktail ceremony to small, culinarily ingenious *dîners*, which entailed corresponding variations in the tape program and her own boudoir *déshabillé*. Only by threats of dire consequences was he able to dissuade her from inviting over a few of her friends, "so they can finally get to know you."

He evaded these *"plaisirs du foyer,"* as she called them, by encouraging her passion for movies whenever she showed signs of demanding a form of togetherness extending beyond what he saw as the primary purpose of their rendezvous. They often watched up to three films an evening, and although this bored him, it had the advantage of relieving him of the necessity of conversation and diverting Denise from any bright ideas about "entertaining." What's more, it kept to a minimum the duration of the parting scene that followed their subsequent caresses in the damask tent, and the postcoital dalliance Denise doted on; in view of the lateness of the hour, he merely planted a brief peck on her forehead as he adjusted his suspenders.

But it turned out Denise was no stranger to the strategy of stubborn resistance. Indefatigably she continued to make plans for a vacation à deux. Miami attracted her less than Honolulu, but from Miami one could fly to Nassau, another long-cherished destination; naturally, at the top of her list of dream trips stood Europe, with protracted visits to Paris, Colmar, and—pinnacle of the cream cake!—a kind of honeymoon in Venice. She gave him hideous ties and was hurt when he didn't wear them. She ignored the often violent irritation he showed whenever she addressed him, in the intimate manner of a long-standing mistress, as the real owner of her apartment ("You really must talk to the super about the heating sometime, dear") in front of the doorman. On the street, she overlooked the way he turned up his collar so high it covered his ears, and the way he bundled her straight into a cab as soon as they were on the sidewalk; and she never voiced amazement at the way he chose movies in theaters miles beyond the zone in which he might have bumped into people he knew. She didn't know that the opinion of these acquaintances was a matter of indifference to him, and that if they had met him in her company, the danger of their reporting it to Linda didn't worry him. Linda hadn't minded his dabbles for a long time; she might even have been gratified to learn that he was finally pursuing his prey in remoter preserves than her circle of immediate friends, as had once bothered her.

To what extent, he asked himself, was Denise's thick skin a matter of policy? Did her pride forbid her acknowledging that he did not want to be seen with her? Certainly he had every reason to be ashamed of his snobbery; it had caused him bitter suffering when he was young and he'd come to despise it, yet the wretched reaction seemed to transcend his moral and aesthetic convictions, being governed by a system of class prejudice not even America had been able to drub out of him.

The awareness of how much he was at the mercy of such

prejudices, such ancient snobberies and unjustified disdains, drove him to the wall, morally speaking. They had molded his character. His attitude to Denise was ambivalent and therefore hypocritical. He didn't know how clever he should deem her. Was her lack of response (feigned or real) to his gruffness and impatience a calculated tactic of attrition? Or did she, out of a compulsive psychological inversion, emphasize and even exaggerate precisely those characteristics that were bound to enrage him?

He detested himself for being so critical, but he suffered terribly every time they went out and she clung to his arm like an organ-grinder's monkey, leaning into him with all her weight. He suffered every time she stopped in front of a big hotel, begged to be taken in for a "little" drink at the bar, and when he gave in, hurled herself upon him by way of thanks. He could have cheerfully socked her when she straightened his tie in front of everyone or jabbed her knuckles in the small of his back as a reminder to sit up straight.

She celebrated an astronomical number of holidays: Christmas and Easter, his birthday, her birthday, the anniversary of the day they met, the inauguration of their love-nest (and the damask tent), the first, second, and third anniversaries of the opening of Chez Denise, all sorts of Catholic holidays, Jewish holidays (since for quite a while she seemed to believe he was a Jew, and was only half convinced when he mildly contested it). At every conceivable chance for festivity, she wished for a romantic supper in a luxury restaurant, the kind of place where he could bank on meeting people he knew, and where she, smiling unctuously, would raise and clink her glass against his each time the waiter refilled it, then snatch at his hand—no matter where it was at that moment—or throw her arms around his neck at the least indication of friendly solicitude. In suburban movie houses she cuddled up to him as if he were a GI on leave and she his one-night stand, allowing her nanny hand free rein in the darkness.

78

His feeling for her fluctuated between deep tenderness and loathing. If her behavior was spontaneous, pure, and naively unself-conscious, then it must melt a heart of stone; if it was method, he had to admire her shrewdness. Also, he was moved by the truth that certain human situations did indeed make such shrewdness indispensable. But one way or the other, she got on his nerves.

She wasn't a tart, and if she accepted what he bestowed upon her (ridiculously little, if one considered his enormous wealth), it was well within acceptable margins. After all, she demanded nothing, asked for nothing, simply took it for granted that the rich man who was her lover made life comfortable for her. Sometimes he told himself that she was innocent enough to have developed a certain fondness for him out of pure gratitude. That she might actually love him, as she claimed to—and often demonstrated in an astonishingly convincing manner—was an idea he permitted himself to entertain only with great reservations.

She was thirty-two years old, thus well past the age in which women traditionally cling to father figures, especially since the nanny-hand game could not compensate in the long run for what a young man might offer her. He had assured her that he wouldn't mind if she slept with other men, but she maintained that that was impossible; not only was she monogamous by nature and religion, but she couldn't imagine experiencing anywhere near the same pleasure with any other partner. This may well have been true—sexuality is rife with these inexplicable paradoxes—yet he was not wholly convinced. He did not find himself worthy of love, and few instances in the past had proved the contrary to him. That, presumably, was why he found it impossible to express tender feelings for her, even when he was touched by something she said or did.

He thought of her now with that twinge of melancholy which emanates from the belly of the world and which, although it paralyzes one's confidence in life with the prick of its pain, contains exquisite consolation: the thought that all things must pass in the end to the monstrous dark whence they issued forth, a tiny spark between two black blocks of eternity, glowed out and extinguished as if it had never existed.

There had to be a way of avoiding, or at least alleviating, a little of this suffering. Even as he felt the impulse to raise his hand and run it through Denise's wood-shaving curls—if only in the most casual and perfunctory way—a resistance would begin, the resistance one feels to a puppy that jumps happily all over one the moment its head is stroked. The reaction was blameworthy, he knew, unforgivably so, for it had nothing to do with the illegitimacy of their relationship or its attendant cautions and precautions. It was the heartlessness of a socially superior being toward a woman from the lower orders. This shamed him all the more deeply since he knew that it came from human nature's crudest animal depths and could be overcome only in a condition of saintliness.

He had grown up in a half-Armenian family in which archbishops and fabulously wealthy merchant princes treated third and fourth cousins—taxi drivers or shepherds who lived with their flocks in fieldstone huts—with the greatest possible consideration, all of them united by the same respect for the human worth of the neighbor, a respect tested and strengthened by pogroms and humiliations. And now here he was, guilty of the arrogance of class. In his youth he had hated the fatuous snobbery of his British schoolmates, which had caused him to commit his first despicable act—of betraying his infantile faith. At times he even despised the cautious, nouveau-riche presumptions of the bridge- and tennis-playing Linda, who pretended to know nothing of the garbage-disposal service on which her father had built his fortune. But none of this helped: at a single incorrectly pronounced word or the excessively refined poising of a fork, a glaringly tasteless dress or the staggering banality of one of Denise's philosophical observations ("Bobby Kennedy could've been the Jesus Christ of the Atomic Age"), he felt himself prickling inside.

Nothing could free him from this spontaneous and uncontrollable hostility, least of all the thought of how hurtful it would be for Denise to learn how or why it came about. On the contrary: it was precisely this thought that drove him to cruelties that hardly admitted any doubt as to the source of his aggression.

He had a set of extenuating arguments to hand, of course. He told himself, for instance, that although he didn't love Denise, he did feel more warmth and affection for her than for Linda, and that must mean something, if he considered that Linda was his lawful wedded wife and that as an Armenian he bore within him an archaic sense of family feeling as deeply rooted as the class prejudices that were the legacy of his English education. Even his occasional malevolent rebellion against the Other, *woman*—the race hatred of men for everything feminine, the old masculine lament of not being able to achieve with loving or beloved women the union of the souls that would make an armistice possible—was more conciliatory in respect to Denise, his judgment of her less cold and cutting. Denise loved, as opposed to Linda, who *was* loved, and that made his feelings for her more poignant.

Yet Linda came out on top. Time and again he would catch himself in little treacheries, ways of sacrificing Denise to her. Sometimes, on an evening when he had flatly refused Denise's request to be taken to dinner at '21', he would invite Linda there. Or after an especially profluent sexual bout with Denise, he felt himself fortified to return home and face the impassively spread thighs of his lawfully wedded wife, where, in a vain attempt to rouse her to some sign of participation, he would stammer into her ear sweet words of love the likes of which would have caused Denise to swoon.

But it would go too far to lay the blame for this disgraceful behavior on his snobbish irritation with Denise's imperfect breeding and media-fed mediocrity. The truth was simpler—and crueler. He loved Linda and not Denise. What was one to do? It was the way of the world, and it was the way of love.

## And Here He Stands, in Distress

His fit of madness this morning had started as a kowtow to his wife, only to wind up as an abstruse form of rebellion against her. He had spent a restless night and then set out, listlessly, on a banal tour of inspection of the Queen of the Sea's churches, palaces, and museums, *Guide bleu* clasped in his hand as befitted a culture consumer, even if he was a scion of one of the moldiest tribes of humanity ever to come from the foot of Mount Ararat. As he filled his eyes with Bellinis (*père et fils*), Carpaccio, Giorgione, Titian, Tintoretto, Veronese, *e tutti quanti*, he realized with increasing annoyance that he was simply expanding the class struggle between the two ladies of his heart into a culture struggle.

This made his flight even more ludicrous. It degraded his motive to the small tragedy of a henpecked husband. There was no panache. He thought of one of those children's guns that noisily fire off a cork at the end of a string. If only he'd been able to flee from his present way of life to some totally different form of existence or at least some other, genuine adventure: to the forests of Brazil or the icy wastes of the Antarctic, where there was still virgin snow (where, indeed?), or the dives of some seedy quayside quarter, anywhere that wasn't entered in Baedeker as "colorful and characteristic and well worth the connoisseur's attention"—at least the corniness would be more palatable.

He was not even really traveling—a tourist, that's what he was! He was allowing himself to be propelled by one of the tides that seasonally move the planet's five-billion-headed, bipedal human multitudes, mass migration, whether hostile or amicable. What wondrous powers unleash and guide such momentous movements? A macabre cultural curiosity. One went from point to point with a view to viewing the past. One passed not only through space but also, above all, through time. A large portion of humanity was perpetually on the move, busy con-

firming its own lack of culture with the example given by something lost, sauntering from one prime exhibit of the vanished
cult to the next. And he sauntered with the best of them, most
intensively here in Venice.

## Hate Thy Neighbor

Naked hatred bubbled inside him. The animosity he felt toward
the hordes of other tourists as they filed past the art treasures
mounted to hysteria. Outside, undulating over every accessible
square inch of terra firma between the ooze of the canals and the
pillars of the propped-up palaces, they were unbearable; inside,
welded into compact blocks in deference to the authority of the
performances they were witnessing, they drove him to thoughts
of gruesome violence. What angered him even more than the
stench of their sweat and the odious commentaries they listened
to was the somatic herd-allegiance that made them—and yes,
him too!—gape at one artistic marvel after another, gawp at the
fetishistic expression of a cult they could neither understand nor
evaluate but whose alien, uncanny holiness they accepted.

## It's Everybody's Fate

He was no different. And he was servile about it too. He wanted
to purge from himself—by continuous meditation on his wife
and constant contemplation of great art—the torrent of images
that his cinematic slumming with Denise had flung at his eyes
and that pierced to the quick of his nervous system. This surfeit
of visual trash had been the apotheosis of his betrayal of Linda
and her aesthetic hygiene, her strict schooling in supreme artistic
achievements from the tombs of the pharaohs to Jasper Johns, a
baser act of unfaithfulness than if he'd spent his time knocking
around with drug addicts and black whores in downtown
honky-tonks. ("At least you have the chance to develop some
sort of style with them," she had once been heard to utter

83

nasally in one of her more epigrammatic moods; this reminded him of Larbaud's deliciously dilettante lines: *Je veux baiser le mépris à pleines lèvres; allez dire à la Honte que je meurs d'amour pour elle. . . .*) His shame was cultural profligacy, and he didn't hesitate to lay the responsibility at Denise's door. Ever since he'd known her, this descent into popular culture had nagged at his conscience. If now, in Venice, he absorbed great art in voracious gulps, as Denise devoured movies, it was a gesture of humility, repentance, spiritually going down on his knees, clutching a votive picture of his wife to his heart, crawling past the stations of the cross in an eminent place of pilgrimage.

But at the same time he felt rebellion welling up inside him. He was being swept along to worship idols and graven images, and Linda was heading there too, riding in the purple gondola of aesthetic high-priestdom and fanned with incense-laden hot air by a retinue of pulp journalists.

## Ecologically Genuine, So to Say

Although Denise wallowed at the very bottom of the communal bog, there was no denying she was independent, honest, candid in her choice, less easily shocked by the idol Art and its attendant cultural clergy. Faced with a Madonna by Giorgione, she might well display the same emotion that made tears trickle down her cheeks at the sight of a Christmas card depicting Aryan blond angels singing "Hallelujah" as comets whizzed about them; or it might have left her cold, in which case no art history lecturer in the world could induce her to abandon her indifference.

This spontaneity made Linda's self-consciously cultivated artistic sense seem empty, like her absentminded passivity in bed compared with Denise's sizzling orgasms. Above all, it revealed him as a hypocritical lip-servicer and moral coward. His cheeks burned when he thought back on those high-class art history lectures at the Metropolitan Museum, with black-tie dinners afterward, which were part of Linda's winter social calendar and at which her mother's bone-chilling vulgarity was matched by the "importance" of her pop art collection. Yet his mother-in-law's ostentatious patronage was more honest—less insipid—than his own behavior here in Venice, where he devoted himself to compulsory aesthetic exercises. In Grandmother's day these docile art trips were a highly esteemed pastime for young ladies of good family; they spilled from the nineteenth century—an era of belief in progress, bursting with educational ambitions—into the Atomic Age, where they were as ludicrously and preposterously out of place as the professorial mortarboards and orange-blossom weddings that figured in Denise's favorite movies as symbols of achieved social success and corollary bliss.

Linda's mother, with her washerwoman tastes, believed in her heart of hearts that avant-garde pictures were a mockery of the idea of beauty and art; nevertheless she acquired them at great expense in order to gain access to the social stratosphere, a world where the more gifted offshoots of European nobility made their living as art lackeys in the auction houses. As a hardened parvenu, she would openly admit that she kept a sharp eye on the cash value of these works; she knew that their putative artistic value was only a kind of cultural bonus, that their constantly rising re-sale value in itself sufficed to elevate her social status.

He of all people should have had a kindred understanding of such cogitations. Instead, he got up on his hind legs and betrayed his own destiny as high priest of the golden calf.

## Which Leads Him Back to the Looking Glass

It was at the Church of Madonna dell'Orto that this thought occurred to him. As he stood there looking up at Tintoretto's *Adoration of the Golden Calf*, his neck muscles tensing, he heard behind him a female voice speaking German, a language he understood only very badly, even though he'd had a German governess. Her cadences aroused his interest. It was a cultured voice, and she was speaking to someone very lovingly, allowing a quality of wonder and mystery to ring through her remarks, as one does when speaking of Christmas to a child.

He made a half-turn, releasing himself from the magic spell of the masterpiece, and glanced discreetly in the direction of the voice. To his surprise there were three people: an elegant middle-aged couple, well-dressed and physically trim, the typically clear faces of the light-skinned blond not yet hardened by the veneer of affluence, open as books and with a beseeching air about them, as though they knew how empty their pages were but could do little toward filling them. The man was wearing a snappily striped club tie. Held steady by the woman's hand resting lightly on his shoulder, their offspring stood between them, an adolescent Mongoloid whose limbs already indicated an alarming growth potential.

He was acutely embarrassed by the sight of this familial tragedy, and even more by the eyes of the parents, which seemed to signal a kind of password, identifying themselves as of his own class, and simultaneously to beg forgiveness and understanding for their misbegotten son. He carried the half-turn through to a full one, away from them, but the confrontation disturbed him profoundly.

The picture of the boy was indelible—a being fated to grow into a powerful man and yet remain forever an ageless, helpless child; his parents, who doubtless loved him, attempted to mollify the biological faux pas with strong doses of art. It was the zenith of cultural conformity. The pitiable creature was a victim of impermissible manipulation, he thought angrily.

## In Come the Clowns

He tried to shake off the almost touching emotions that the boy's puffy face, knoblike nose, and tender, childish mouth aroused in him. But he was spellbound by the poetry in the sunken, keenly attentive bearing of the head, to which the soft, blond, brushed-shining child's hair gave an air of something precious; and by the wondering expression in the large, almond-shaped, slightly protruding, heaven-clear eyes, which didn't look but which saw without seeing—nothing in particular, no definable objects, most definitely not the painting in front of them, no, just saw, even as the listening was directed at nothing in particular, yet keenly attuned to the inner voices of the world.

It seemed to him a base profanity to parade a person of such unsullied purity in front of this archaic overvalued junk, before all these pricey products established by the collective need of faith, these exhibitionistic top performances; circus acts of art proficiency, miracles of life pretense; all the exalted drama, high-mindedness, nobility, passion, courage, chasteness, humility, and God knows what other legendary virtue-promulgating artifacts produced by the daubing and chipping lackeys of secular and clerical powers. It was all aimed to achieve the rat-catching of souls: if no longer for a God or a Church then for the idol Art (and with it, the great idol Money). What a lack of common sense, what sheer brainlessness of the parents to expose the unfortunate cretin to such questionable attractions. Why not go straight to Lourdes?

## Owning Up to the Trivial

He had continued his pilgrimage along the stations of the cross of the glorious Venetian past, now with the outrageously dark and triumphant feeling of one who is about to celebrate a black mass. It tickled his ironic fantasy that his trusty travel guide dispensed between one and three stars to hostelries, high-class eateries, and works of art alike, according to the alleged quality each had to offer. Why not similarly grade one's sightseeing duties? One could judge one's own performance and award oneself marks for diligent accomplishment of a set curriculum.

He enjoyed counting up the number of stars he accumulated

with each viewed masterpiece, to see just how close he could get to the dream mark awarded those happy few who went the full cultural distance. Sightseeing no longer in order to assimilate culture but in order to assimilate stars, he reduced Linda, his mother-in-law, and the whole kit and caboodle of culture tourists to a common denominator. Left over, as irrational imponderables, so to speak, were Denise and the retarded boy.

By the time he got to one hundred stars he was sick of the game. With a snarl of disgust he propelled the *Guide bleu* into the moss-green waters of the Canal Grande.

This grim burst of humor afforded him something like freedom. By the time he made his way by *vaporetto* back to his hotel on one of the lagoon islands, he had, for the first time on this fugitive's global circumnavigation, plucked up enough courage to look in the eye the humiliating circumstances that had started it.

## Shame on Us All

It had been one of those weekends in Southampton that he hated and for which he nonetheless had prepared himself with perverse thoroughness. Out of a stubborn refusal to behave as would be expected of him, he performed with self-inflicted cruelty the sabbatical attitudes of a middle-class businessman. Perfectly decked out for sojourn in the pioneer house among the cart wheels, powder horns, and bird decoys, he had gone to buy provisions at Zabar's. Linda, who never fathomed his irony in doing so, gladly left this chore to him and waited in the parked car reading a newspaper. And although he realized that each minute spent dawdling in front of the delicatessen's bounteous counters could mean at least a half-hour's difference in the Friday-afternoon traffic (he could have gone to Southampton by helicopter), he hemmed and hawed while choosing among various kinds of smoked salmons, caviars, pastramis, smoked reindeer and bear hams, Greek and Turkish olives, goat and sheep cheeses, corn and rye breads, and other groceries to go with the wrought-iron weather vane and open-fire pots of his Early American cottage. It was a sort of revenge, though perceived only by him.

But here again he betrayed Denise, on whose culinary finesse he haughtily turned a cold shoulder, and who, had she seen this hamper of myriad delicacies, would have had paroxysms. In front of this hoard of food, stockpiled to assuage some aesthetic gluttony, born of a subconscious allegiance to greed, he sensed once again the insistent but slippery feeling that he was taking part in a despicable, collective offense.

## Home

Linda's usual leisure-time guests awaited them at the pioneer house, the same artists and journalists, cushioned within the same cozy group of chic social outriders who rallied under Linda's leadership; he'd shocked all of them. The elegant fops were beyond discussion, and there was little love lost between him and the writers and journalists he mistrusted. The intellectuals were secretly would-be politicians, he thought, and their interest in spiritual matters seemed to be marked by frustration—and rage—over the powerlessness of the spirit. And the artists, in their eager readiness to commit any kind of violence, reminded him of Russian anarchists in the far-off days of the Tsars, their destructive bent channeled into aestheticism.

He detested his weekend garb—also chosen in bitter irony (for he had hoped that in this, at least, Linda would see how phoney their performance was): faded blue tight-fitting studded pants, ridiculous cowboy boots, and hideous red-and-black-checked lumberman's jacket; and he loathed it doubly because it resembled the outfits of their guests. Their moth-eaten lambskin jackets and nautical caps, sewer-cleaner's gum boots and polar explorer's parkas were combat uniforms, knights' raiment for a ludicrous cultural crusade: they had set out to challenge the world, to make it into a better, freer, fuller one; they were supported by their women in nostalgic governess nightshirts, feather boas, gypsy fortune-teller head-scarves, and malkin bodices. In fact they had no notion as to how such a better, freer, fuller world should look, and fell back on the fancy dress of a nineteenth-century bohemia of the worst kind. What they achieved was nothing but a more and more generalized coarsening of the world. Contributing to this beggars' opera, he betrayed his class as well as his convictions—himself, in other words. He did it on purpose: It all led to a paradoxical conjecture that nothing escaped the clutches of conformity anymore; everything was doomed to one treachery or another.

## Liberation

On Saturday evening, in front of a blazing open fire, everything came to the top, like the results of an overindulgence in indigestible food. It had been an unusually cold day, but still it seemed strange to gather in front of a fire in August; all part of the communal weekend spirit, he told himself resignedly. The guests were spread easily around the living room as though its pioneer austerity were their natural habitat, as though they'd just gotten back from an exhausting turkey hunt with a few Indian scalps dangling from their belts. One of them, a fellow he found especially unsympathetic, an athletic nature boy with a banana-colored Tarzan mane and a Mafia boss's name who fabricated works of art from tree trunks, railway lines, and rocks, poured himself a tumblerful of very expensive Swiss plum schnapps and drank it in one gulp. In those bygone halcyon days when he himself had sought the stimulating, spiritualizing effects of alcohol (albeit never in the John Wayne, Western-saloon style; rather, as a member of Esseintes's retinue in Huysmans's *À rebours*), this mighty swig would have impressed him, and he would have admired the fool's capacity to hold his booze. But now his aversion was violent, and he did something quite contrary to his usually generous nature. He got up, went over to the bottle, recorked it, and replaced it ostentatiously on the highest shelf of the liquor cabinet. In turning back, he stumbled—the high heels of his boots, no doubt—over a very precious early-eighteenth-century perambulator, a gem in Linda's collection. The thin wheel-spokes bent under his weight like reeds buckling beneath a reclining rhinoceros.

It conformed to the lamentable rules of the game that he should now vent his wrath on his wife.

"What on earth is all this junk doing in the house anyway?" he barked at her. "Do we have a child, or a grandchild, to lay in this spider's chariot? If we did I'd forbid this object from the word go. What in heaven's name are we? Pilgrim fathers? Quaker progeny? Just what is this big production number going on? Are we trying to prove we're really and truly Americans? That we're doing our best to erase our real roots? To rid our genes of all the dirt—is that it? Beat all the darkness out of ourselves, what? Accentuate the Frisian and Celtic aspects, even though our forefathers were as Oriental as the Three Wise Men? They weren't bear hunters or whale fishermen, they peddled their way here with rag bundles on their backs! Why don't we live what we are? In suitable surroundings? Instead of the Versailles nonsense in town and the Walden setup here in the country, we could go in for Early Jewish, for instance—what do you say? Why don't you lead interior design along the Yellow Brick Road again and proclaim the shtetl style to be the ne plus ultra of fashionable furnishings? Chagall as a designer, hmmm? The household as a mobile possession, ready to be loaded on a cart at the drop of a hat, with a cockerel and a trumpet sitting on top! Why don't—"

He broke off as one of the artists' squaws threw herself on his neck and warbled, "Oh, Aram, you're wonderful. You're just a genius. I simply must kiss you!"

He thrust her rudely away, went to the telephone in his bedroom, and phoned his secretary, who was at his permanent beck and call, to book an open plane ticket for him first thing in the morning. On Monday night he flew off into the blue.

## Slipped on a Slip

Okay, so the blockheads surmised a marital crisis and would hold him to be a hitherto camouflaged anti-Semite. Fine by him. Linda, ever since the '67 war, had proudly taken to stressing her Jewishness and getting on his nerves with it. His own case was not without a certain piquant flavor. In his profession he was surrounded more by Jews than non-Jews and was generally looked on as one of them. He never corrected this assumption. He might just as well have been half Jewish as half Armenian; Armenians and Jews belonged to the oldest and most dignified races on earth and were the most conspicuous victims of genocide in history. And when he thought of his aunts' cucumber noses it seemed silly to make a distinction. As an Armenian, he felt the racial characteristics common to both races, as alike as two peas.

## Strange Deviation

He knew that with this identification he was guilty of disloyalty to the traditional attitude of his Armenian countrymen, who were anything but well disposed toward Jews. But he went even further and encouraged people to take him for a Jew. It tickled his irony to provoke this egg dance in people who hated him racially but revered his riches. It amused him to observe their relief upon hearing that he wasn't a Jew after all, and to watch the dampening of their premature delight as it then dawned on them that as an Armenian he wasn't persona grata either. Their dissembling courteousness and forced tactfulness rapidly changed into a kind of gallows intimacy. ("I can't think why I thought you belonged to the chosen people—probably because there are hardly any of us left in the world of finance, are there? Haha!")

He was well acquainted with the humiliation of race and class prejudice not only from his school days among the blond, kidney-pudding British. Even the checkered cosmopolitan sidewalks of New York were not swept entirely clean of it. The artists and journalists in Linda's circle might pride themselves on their philo-Semitism, but it was all a put-on; thus it delighted him that they, who had taken him for a Jew, should now be shaken by a crass example of Jewish anti-Semitism. The idiot child's German parents would doubtless have soundly confirmed many a preconceived opinion here.

Could it have been this ambiguity, which made his outburst confusing for him, that caused him to flee? Of course the impulse to run away from himself, to turn his back on the whole routine with all its trappings, wasn't original. Such things were looked on as natural, symptoms of a peculiar state of age and health. No, his moral lapse had other sources and verged on other zones, which even with the help of a psychiatric shaman would be difficult to decode.

He thought back on it with a feeling of superstitious awe. Certainly he'd not intended to refer to either Linda's Jewishness or his own Armenianness when he spoke of ridding their genes of dirt; rather, he'd expressed something linked to the premonitions of death that he was loath to put into words.

## Metaphysical Meandering

It was something he could phrase only very clumsily, something eccentric, absurdly against reason. Anyway, it went far beyond a rift between two souls in one breast. The lifelong submerged feeling was that his own I, the specific structure of his own individuality, was his own worst enemy, that it hindered him in opening and expanding out beyond himself. By holding onto an image of himself as a singular person, rock-solid in the wholeness of life, a single, unique occurrence in the universe, he felt he was thwarting his chances of stepping out-

93

side himself and becoming one with the world. At certain moments—above all now, at life's end, when the past called to him like an echo of himself from a forgotten time and world—his belonging to a whole was almost physically prevented by the treacherous transparent casing that enclosed what he'd always believed was himself. In fact it was nothing but an imprinted image of that self, a fancy based on various paradigms determined by shifting spirits of the time. You could see clearly which of the patterns suggested by these shifts had formed which fancies; in spite of the supposed individual's isolation, his relationship to the whole can be recognized easily—yet hopelessly set apart, made redundant by being locked within itself, mute as a message in a bottle with no meaning but sweet nothings.

## Keep Secrets to Yourself

These thoughts—or rather, feelings, sentiments—had proliferated in the romantic phase of his youth and had then, naturally, receded in the immediacy of everyday adult life. But not completely. He had nurtured them secretly and wasn't surprised when they popped up now so intensely. The confusing thing was the vehemence with which his youth presented itself as a period of purity and innocence. Yes, of course, his childhood had been spent in passionate faith in the reality of heaven and hell. But soon after, he'd played out his adventures of the soul far beyond the domain of the metaphysical without noticing any deficiencies; not to mention the later years, of course, dedicated to the exciting game of making money.

What a kettle of fish! Now, on top of neurotic crises, premonitions of death, and lapses such as his tirade against Linda and the hell-for-leather flight from New York, he was developing a tendency to mystic speculation, capable of transporting him to deliriums (as that afternoon in Manhattan, at Madison Square, where he'd suddenly seen himself as God's bard). With this kind

94

of thing going on, he ran the risk of being called to appear as a prosecution witness, so to speak, for the tritest platitudes of Linda's journalists. Of all the secret deviations from the mythic image of the Wall Street shark he projected in public, a relapse into early puberty was the last thing he wanted to have come to their attention.

Especially the experience he'd had in Vienna.

## Rising of a New Star

The decision to include Vienna in his itinerary was another spontaneous idea—it happened only because (if he remembered rightly) he saw the word VIENNA by accident at the Rome airport. He'd watched NEW YORK, OSLO, CARACAS, HAMBURG, MADRID, SAN FRANCISCO, CAPE TOWN flicking on a gray-white TV screen, watched how with each new departure they'd leaped and interchanged like the digits on his Japanese wristwatch. Suddenly VIENNA was there, and he asked himself in astonishment what the old operetta metropole was doing in this slick geographical crap game.

He didn't know Vienna at all. Yes, he'd pulled in and out of its railway station countless times on his way to school in England. For him it was the pivotal point between the two halves of his being: when he traveled from Braila, Vienna was the first city of the civilized West; when he came back from London, it was the first city of the Balkans. This way or that, that way or this, Vienna was a go-between, a sort of hiatus between two realities. It was part of a submerged world. Even now he could remember the myriad colors of a newsstand projected against the sooty, dark gray of the main platform, where clouds of white steam swirled all about. He used to stock up there on chocolate, oranges, magazines, crossword puzzle booklets, and other diversions for the journey. . . . But no, could he swear to it? On second thought, it might have been Innsbruck, or Strasbourg. . . . The stops had never been long enough to allow him

95

to poke his nose into the town proper; and perhaps also Vienna already seemed more a myth than a tangible reality.

## Reality, at Last

Now here it was, a city that still existed, integrated in the international flight network. The Vienna of the two-headed eagle and the poly-peopled Central Europe between the wars had a present! Was something of those other worlds left there? Could he escape the uniform plastic atmosphere of the worldwide hotel chain here?

He needed three days to recover from the dismal shock that this beautiful, malicious, provincial metropolis dressed up as an imperial charnel house dealt him. Death was generally considered something nocturnal; he always imagined it darkly draped. Vienna's dead Baroque and *Gründerzeit* glories were spread out in broad daylight beneath a blue heaven, dry as bones and lit by the sun like those grave niches of a southern Italian *camposanto*. Rolling waves of generation after generation of Europeans had washed up cultural driftwood on its shores and then sucked it down again in the backwash. What remained was a beachcomber depot, an antique storehouse of cracked and moldy cultural gems. Fanning it all was a glacier wind that carried with it the scent of alpine meadows and fir forests, pungently flavored with urban smog and exhaust fumes, out toward the Great Nothing that, now yawning in the East, had once dazzled with color, vibrated with vitality, fiddled exuberantly and piously as a shepherd: the other half of his European home.

## Schubert's Requiem

He checked into an old guesthouse on a narrow, gray, cobblestoned side street off Kärntnerstrasse. The hotel was indeed a relic of the Middle Ages, with an abundance of florid barococo plus a touch of incongruous Schubertiana, a solid house with stout walls to which he scurried home every evening—after long days dutifully gathering impressions—like a frightened animal to its burrow.

On the evening before his departure, he returned from Schönbrunn Palace deeply irritated. He'd spent the afternoon like a madman in a phantom world; he found himself dwarfed by a dream perspective of huge treetops cut at right angles to converge, raylike, on the vanishing point of a pavilion perched on top of a hill: the empty aerie of a mythical two-headed eagle awaiting its landlord's return. The sky above was of the same gentle dusty pale-blue as the crumbling canopies above the palace beds, which still held the impressions of the bodies of those who'd once slept there. Ever more oppressed now by his dwarf-likeness and the ominous proximity of his own death, he wandered through incredibly long and empty corridors, went upstairs, downstairs, through rooms and chambers full of rickety gilded furniture, fragile porcelain, and sun-bleached damasks, past laid tables at which the deceased apparently still supped at the witching hour, through nurseries containing cradles for children who'd been moldering in their graves for centuries now, into stables with bridles for phantom horses and coach houses full of ghostly carriages.

## God's Hideout

His frayed nerves suffered a final blow on the way back to town, where the mushroom-hatted natives in their German diesel cars cavorted in the rush-hour traffic like Ben Hurs driving four-in-hands of oxen. His hotel was in a pedestrian zone, so he had his cab drop him at the end of Kärntnerstrasse and then picked his way on foot through hordes of promenading tourists from behind the Iron Curtain, petty pensioners, Gypsies, and beggar students torturing musical instruments, till he could slip into the narrow side street flanked by palaces decorated with coats of arms and idle boutiques. A few steps from his hotel, a small door in one of the massive portals opened suddenly, silently, beside him and a smell of incense wafted out. He caught a glimpse of oil lamps glowing in the dark interior.

What had made him so curious? A mere impulse, by now automatic, to view anything that came within his ken? He'd killed a goodly amount of time this way. He turned back and went in.

## Curiosity Rewarded

He was standing in the vault of a kind of cloister church, whose luscious Baroque he sensed more than saw, so impenetrable was the grotto's purple darkness. Only when his eyes grew accustomed to the gloom did its contents come into view, by the light of the flickering gleam of candles before the altar and along the walls, reflected in the varnish of the great gold-framed oil paintings and the shiny wooden pews, polished by the use of centuries. He dimly made out the rear aspects of several old women, kneeling or sitting. Apart from a faint shuffling that sounded whenever one of them moved or scurried away, or when a new one, bowing, entered sheepishly, semi-curtsied and hastily crossed herself, and sidled in her onion layers of black clothing into one of the pews, it was quite still; and the stillness took hold of him in an odd way.

It was an extraordinarily rich and one might almost say relaxed, patrician stillness; stillness in its full glory, resting in itself, drinking of itself to the fill. Neither the absence of noise, bustle, disquiet, nor the opposite of these, but rather existing as though for itself alone, autarkic, sovereign. It was different from any other kind of stillness he could remember, and it filled the high, narrow church vault as fully as the purple darkness, which now gradually seemed pleasantly velvetlike, drenched in the gold of the crowns and the bloodred of the billowing gowns in the sacred pictures. The soft scraping and scratching of the praying women, the muffled footfalls as they came and went didn't break the stillness; on the contrary, these made it seem even more consolidated, intimate, pacifying.

## Trapped

A small voice insinuated to him that this stillness might well be so rich and authoritarian because of the accumulated reverence of appeased souls present in this space—but no, he couldn't accept this grossly materialistic notion, it was not so. The stillness was far more mysterious than that, far more mystical. *It,* the stillness itself, appeased; it engendered reverence. Something in it raised it above the prayers of the devout. It was exalted by timelessness. It contained eternity.

He felt a wave of fury rise in him. It was as though he'd caught himself at something unworthy: something that offended spiritual hygiene; something disreputably seductive that he should forbid himself, like the erotic fantasies he'd sought to fortify himself with in order to fulfill his murderous marital copulation curriculum. A tempter was lurking here in the cryptic murmur of sumptuous darkness, in the stillness steeped in shades of eternity. He knew him and his impossible promises well. With the same obstinacy with which he bedded his wife despite no prospect of metaphysical success, he determined to resist this temptation to relinquish his reason.

His restlessness doubled and trebled. The incense tore at his throat. Noisily he left the old hags' place of worship. It would have pleased him to slam the great portal behind him, but the mighty heave he gave it was cushioned by a pneumatic stopper. It closed off the stillness from him as silently as it had admitted him to it.

## Art, the Tempter

The fury stayed. He had carried it about ever since, had brought it here to Venice. It bubbled covertly, like a geyser; above it hung the poison fumes of his sarcasm, his desperation, his

99

pent-up emotions. He'd sensed the fury brimming as swarms of tourists charged raucously through the churches and crowded out-of-the-way chapels on lonely back canals, with their hairy limbs, obscene breasts, towering knapsacks and tent poles; he was upset, he told himself sardonically, because he'd secretly hoped to find the same stillness here in Venice that he'd encountered in Vienna. He hated himself for his sentimentality.

To ease the pain, he sharpened his lookout for every profanation of the sacred. In San Marco he gloated over the barbarian squads gaping there, pushing each other along like sheep as though it were a fairground. They were right, of course: The basilica was a Byzantine bazaar, never a house of God. He himself began frolicking like a naughty boy. He laughed with undisguised scorn at a monsignor with a banker's face who approached him on the quayside near Santa Maria della Salute dressed perfectly in the style of the theatrical backdrop of gondolas and humpbacked bridges over the Canal Grande—a Carnival figure.

The priest's astonished glance did not bring him to his senses. He now began to identify Venice with the Church—the Church he had hated since losing his childish faith. If the skyscrapers stretching to the golden sun in Madison Square had appeared like a gigantic temple construction of God-yearning, then the fretwork Gothic of the Venetian palazzi—their reflections in the water like the upside-down images of playing-card figures— seemed a clever theater production, cunningly staged to catch the precious souls who were so quick on the draw with their pocketbooks (not only in church).

He suspected a metaphysical plot against him. All the beauty handed down from the past, all the great art, all the noble traces of high culture were clubbing together to trick him. The daubing and chipping stooges of the Church and aristocracy had done their work well. He had once gladly turned his back on this old continent; now it was duping him into thinking he'd left something behind that was irreplaceably important. More than just his youth. More than the world of that epoch—anything but healthy, true, but oh so much easier to live in, so reckless, elegant, and substantial! No, no: It was a matter of his cultural identity and therefore his spiritual well-being—or vice versa.

## Big, Wide, Empty World

The earlier part of his journey, which had taken him to Japan and India, had gone off without a hitch. He went sightseeing there as well, of course, but most of it had seemed insignificant. Except for some astonishing sand sculptures in the temple gardens of Kyoto and a few admirable specimens of adroit handwork, some picturesque scenes and landscapes here and there, nothing was so beautiful, interesting, adventurous as his fantasy of the East, fed on picture postcards since early childhood. The mystery of India left him cold. Asia too was full of decorative decay, no lack of monuments to a great past. And there too—more than anywhere!—the antithesis between its dignity and accomplishment and the barbarity of a civilization sold on technology was sickening. But it wasn't *his* affair. In that hurly-burly of Chevrolets and holy cows, money-grubbing dealers and people starving on the street, cripples like medieval curses, fakirs and poor little rich boys and girls—flipped out permanently and questing for the next ashram where they could relieve themselves of whatever vestiges of money and common sense they still possessed—yesterday was so innately interwoven with today that one hardly noticed the seam.

## Time and Space

But the closer he came to his origins and, with them, himself, the more tangibly he began to feel the seam within himself. In Cairo he happened on one of the great historical mosques, towering out of a mass of corrugated-iron shacks in a colony of fellahin. A group of English people of the cultivated kind—two youthful gents in their late sixties with ascetics' Adam's apples and sages' flowing snow-white hair, the one big and bony, the other small and wiry like a jockey, both accompanied by interchangeable, post-climacteric better halves and a single mammoth daughter—were viewing the weathered, destitute building alongside him. They made no attempt to lower their voices, as these were already by nature well tempered and moderate in volume and mixed melodiously with the pigeons' cooing up under the dome. The echo and counterecho of these two sound textures served as a yardstick with which to measure the great dimensions of the room and its emptiness. The beauty of the architecture was awe-inspiring. Great centuries had made manifest in stone something akin to the stillness he later encountered in Vienna and again sought vainly in Venice: eternity translated into terms of space.

While the British raised their watery blue eyes to the chandeliers and exchanged well-informed comments on the items displayed (he was irked by the one professing that the silver ostrich eggs on the chandelier chains had been placed to discourage rats from climbing down and drinking the oil in the lamps), a man came in off the street, a man in rags but not a beggar, a poor man, robust, with the quick secure steps of the diligent. He didn't glance in their direction, didn't see them at all. From among the folds of his rags he extracted the rudiments of a carpet, spread it on the pigeon-bespattered stone floor, knelt down and sternly discharged his silent prayer, briskly, repeatedly bowing in the direction of Mecca, bringing his forehead to touch the floor gently with the expertise of someone who has practiced the selfsame exercise morning, noon, sunset, and night since early childhood. When he was finished and stood up again, something hardly credible came to light—he had grown, visibly, quite a bit. He stood there in the room larger, straighter, more erect than he'd been before. One no longer saw his rags, one saw the upright devotion. He'd been completely self-contained from the start, in all his indigence, an honest man living in the values of humanity, against which the scholarship of the Englishmen seemed forced, presumptuous, silly. He didn't presume. With measured movements he rolled his carpet together and stepped back from his communion onto the sunlit street. He left the mosque cleansed, untouched by their presence, as if their contaminations could affect neither him nor the house of God.

## Thirsty Soul

Envy was an emotion that fate had spared him up to now. It was time to get to know it.

Up to now even his internal battle between light and dark had not made him envious of those who had no such conflict. That the sight of a man praying should acquaint him with envy seemed to him a lame joke, a trick in questionable taste played on him by the malevolent powers of destiny, which seemed to be making it their business to increase his confusion.

But then, it wasn't really such a bad kind of envy, not yet at any rate. For the moment it was a mixture of admiration and longing, close to love, and with this intoxicating adolescent feeling fizzing inside him he measured the degree of dignity the Splendid One in Rags had over him and over the whole enlightened Occident. Only later, after Vienna and the fury triggered there, after that surfacing of completely inexplicable emotions, and above all after the disgust at this morning's farce, did his envy become vicious.

Everything he had viewed recently—all those splendid and yet humble faith-palaces with their dramatic pictorial gems, those masterpieces created in dedication to God while striving to escape the slaughterhouse world and attain celestial bliss, all those testimonies of allegiance to Him in the midst of a world scourged by plagues, wild religious wars, and the indulgence of secular and holy princes—all these things aimed to inform him that the time in which they had been created had been more blessed, "motivated by a more oriented life-feeling," as Linda's journalists put it, "with greater depth and the simultaneous ability to achieve more sublime, more enriching spiritual elevation. . . ."

## See Clearly

That was just another way of demonstrating the jaded cultural pessimism with which the European intelligentsia had preened itself in his youth and which today lived on as common property in the lowlands of popular intellectual life. Someone made a buck on it, a pretty fat one at that. The culture drivel—especially the apocalyptic kind—fed not only the feuilletonists and (even better) their bosses, the book and magazine publishers, but the entire art and antique business and much more besides. If he'd ever doubted it—which he never had, never for an instant—then after visiting a cultural junk shop such as Venice, it could hardly be denied that along with the turgid feelings "Great Art" unleashed in people and the bitter tears they shed on being confronted with the dissolution of the Occident, there arose also a desire to sell it out. Blackmail was accomplished with threats and promises, and an army of intimidated people parted with their money just as trustingly for art as they had once tucked it into the church collecting box. Okay. He was placing himself in the same category when he envied a simple Arab fellah the possibility of combining physical gymnastics with spiritual hygiene; his show of emotion in Cairo sprouted from the same roots as the indignation that befell him on seeing the Germans' idiot son under the Tintoretto in Venice.

Emotions awakened by a confrontation with the stillness of eternity could be channeled productively. There could be a sublime application of what psychologists call transference. But you couldn't catch him with it. He knew too much about it.

## Let's Come to One Point

Once more he thought of the brochure he'd picked up from the hall porter's desk. The company it advertised was born of the money-making spirit—a spirit to which mankind was completely and unanimously oriented. It interested him to see how effectively they'd employed the techniques of transference and rat-catching. Maliciously he told himself that this might help him on his quest for self-knowledge; he would be taking a look in the mirror, not just a coincidental, passing one, as on his way to the bathroom. The person he wanted to meet was his real, true self—behind the myths of the frustrated poet and the predator troglodyte.

He rose from his sweat-soaked bed to a more dignified vertical position and cast an eye about for the booklet. He found it on the table in front of the window overlooking the pool. The moment he saw it he was seized by the same impatience he experienced in his dentist's waiting room. The ads metastasizing in the periodicals he picked through while he nervously anticipated the impending handiwork shortly to be done in the interior of his skull had the common aim of simulating a world "motivated by a more oriented life-feeling, with greater depth and the simultaneous ability to achieve more sublime, more enriching spiritual elevation," whether these ads were selling modes of transport, toilet water, whiskey, gymnastics, or an innovative type of brassiere. The promises were made with primitive methods and an implied sneer that without these blessings one belonged to an underprivileged, inferior genus. The example he now held in front of himself wasn't exactly sublime, he muttered to himself acidly.

## Why Not Join Them?

He began to study the brochure with the interest of a professional, as if it had been submitted to him for inspection by the director of one of his companies. He gleaned nothing new from the sparse text. A maritime company (whose owners, managing directors, worth, and solvency were vaguely known to him) had finally achieved the idea of once again running the legendary Orient-Express on the London–Venice route. News of this enterprise had been haunting the newspapers for years now, yet there'd been but little talk about it in the financial world, merely some skeptical shaking of heads—but this only served to make the psychological aspect of the ad even more interesting.

The brochure's layout was much the same as that used in ads for fashion houses, certain perfumes, luxury hotels and watering places: a language of images designed to appeal to the largest possible audience as members of the elite, to address the likes of Denise and purport to introduce them to an experience befitting their exclusiveness. The slick color photos were meant to reproduce the atmosphere of the late twenties and early thirties—and this concerned him directly and personally, one might say. The promise of the "Great Journey" had been part of his own most ardent and insistent expectations of life, *ce voyage d'été à l'ombre de la fumée du navire,* a voyage on which nothing occurred other than the sensation that one was forever heading for some extraordinary encounter, something indeterminate, something that subtly revealed itself in the language of gestures and the contours of a momentary situation: a woman's arm rising to adjust the decorative arrangement of her coiffure; the nonchalance with which a fur was allowed to slip from naked shoulders; the elegant austerity of a gentleman in a gray topper, field glasses dangling from his shoulder as he instructed his jockey at the racetrack. . . .

He knew the insatiable longing that devoured images such as these for no reason in particular. Whether or not one achieved the "more oriented life-feeling" was a matter of conjecture. It was also a matter of degree, and Linda's cult of "living with art" could not be looked on as the highest. There was no question of mystical God-happenings here, thank the Lord. This was solely a matter of profitably satisfying an apparently prevalent superego need—in other words, of filling a market gap, nothing more.

## That's My Style

He admired the adroitness of the speculation. Rat-catching at its best. And no one could accuse the ads of being misleading. The advertisement for "high society's luxury train" made an appeal not to those who believed they already belonged to an elite, but to those who dreamed of one day being able to join it. If Mrs. Soakes were to complain that on the Orient-Express she'd bumped into none other than Mrs. Noakes and Mr. Boakes, it was still nothing compared with the number of dream addicts who would see in Mr. Boakes, Mrs. Noakes, and yes, even Mrs. Soakes herself fable figures exuding the charisma of the Old World. Mr. B. and the ladies N. and S., all got up in paint and regalia and prancing on the warpath to Belonging, would look as the dreamers imagined the passengers on the Orient-Express to have always looked.

*Prête-moi ton grand bruit, ta grande allure si douce, ton glissement nocturne à travers l'Europe illuminée, O train de luxe! . . .* He'd fallen for this hocus pocus himself in his youth. Already by then the train of the crowned and uncrowned Balkan princes and adventurers of both sexes had long since become the favored means of transport for bourgeois timber merchants and aging courtesans. If Larbaud had sung, *L'angoissante musique qui bruit le long de tes couloirs de cuir doré tandis que derrière des portes laquées, aux loquets de cuivre lourd dorment les millionaires,* then the singer of Barnabooth's experiences had already, with poetic *grandezza,* ignored the fact that the millionaires of his day were of the kind one imagined as languishing behind iron bars rather than brass-ornamented sliding doors; not to mention the hustlers and underworld figures a generation later, to which he himself belonged.

Today's millionaires didn't even have this piquant notoriety to recommend them. Their respectable mugs were better suited to a jumbo jet's synthetic upholstery than to the Jugendstil foliage climbing over the armrests of the saloon car, or the immaculate mess jackets of the stewards on this antediluvian train; they looked a lot better strapped to airline seats and gaping up at stewardesses with cellophane-wrapped sex appeal serving them plastic beakers of Coca-Cola and bags of peanuts. The three-quarters of a century that had elapsed since Larbaud wrote had brought another kind of people to the train.

## Good Shot

The cultural gradient between 1920 and 1980 played no part in calculating the company's chances of success with a "dream journey on the world's most famous luxury train." There was no need for false pretenses. Company and customer were in close mutual rapport. Those ready to dream expected from the dream suppliers nothing more than a dream; children playing a game of ring-around-the-rosy don't expect that riding on Rilke's white elephant or a giant dragonfly will be anything more than a silver-lined fantasy stolen from the cold world of trivial realities.

What counted was the credibility of the dream vehicle, and in this the company had delivered the goods. It had salvaged the old cars from a junkyard somewhere and refurbished them at fabulous expense. Special decorators schooled in art history worked with archaeological precision to ascertain the origins of the velvet of the seats, the glass of the lamps, the porcelain of the washbasins and chamber pots, and then to reproduce and renew everything. The uniforms of the conductors, stewards, and waiters could not, at any time, have made a smarter impression. Bronze and brass workers faithfully copied the solid knobs and locks of the doors behind which everyone could now dream, each to his own taste and inclination, be it as millionaire or gay Lothario, duchess or high-class whore, murderer or appointed

108

victim. In the transparent black of the wide windows, the reflections of the little table lamps, gleaming damask, sparkling glass, and glinting silver slid through the dusky landscape in stylistic purity; in turn, the landscape loomed back through the glass darkly, like a dimly flowing watermark. The freshly polished mahogany, cherry, and rosewood paneling in the sleeping, buffet, and saloon cars shone; white-haired artists of marquetry were found among the almost extinct brotherhood of cabinetmakers to renew the decaying Jugendstil and Art Deco medallions . . . and one of these, reproduced as a decorative ornament between two blocks of text in the brochure, hit the bull's-eye of his senses.

Like the first bars of an old beloved melody, the calling of a word, the wafting of a scent one had thought long faded (or the taste of a madeleine dipped in tea, as the man said), which then become the hallmark of an epoch, he experienced a total recall and felt the alarming, immediate presence of his own youth. How powerful this presence had been, how powerful life-presence is at any time, how powerlessly one is carried along by its current—losing it, moment by moment, to the past, losing oneself with each outlived life-moment.

## The Strength of Despair

He didn't think this, he felt it—or rather, he knew it all at once, by means of one of those inspirations that come from the primeval depths of inherited life-knowledge and are the very last connection we have to those depths, links that occur only rarely and are independent of our willpower. Equally present with his lost lifetime was his death. Just as in dreams two separate conditions often flow together into one, each transparently contained in the other, so too the consciousness of illusion was contained in the momentarily recaptured world of that time, its breath of life suddenly wafted back and, with it, the knowledge of how he'd breathed it then. Not the unrealness of things past, for the moment more real than the present, but the recognition that it had never really happened and that the presence of the here and now was also nothing but a specter.

## Yield!

Never before had he believed himself capable of grasping so clearly the nature of that which is called *time*: the constantly stationary *Totentanz* of tirelessly disintegrating seconds, minutes, hours, days, moons, years; the ceaselessly immobile piling up of the past; the falling back of decades, centuries, millennia, hundreds of thousands, millions of years and their sinking sightlessly into the monstrous space-blackness of eternity; the traceless passing and dissolution of all that likewise ceaselessly and tirelessly emerged from it; the continual will-o'-the-wisp illusions of life in myriad existences flaring up only to fizzle out again immediately, as though they'd never been there in the first place.

There was something in opposition to all forms of life—an omnipotent lifelessness and stillness behind it all. Was it this that pious people were at such pains to communicate with when they prayed, whether shyly scurrying in, squeezing themselves into a pew, and kneeling, or performing calisthenics under a temple's lofty domes, prancing around a totem pole, or contemplating their belly buttons at the foot of the Himalayas? Or even by serving God as money-grubbing slaves among the skyscrapers of Manhattan? . . .

It took more than mere enlightenment to resist populating the holy stillness behind the specter of life with idols, there where the golden calf had been grazing happily for so long. It took mighty resolution to resist the tempter; his aim was to induce one to spirit away the nullity of one's own existence by jettisoning it in the great void—much as one projects a shadow, grotesquely magnified and diffusely mystical, against a swirling screen of fog, then jumps up startled when, for a moment, it looks like God Himself standing there.

He picked up the telephone and asked the hall porter to book him a ticket to London on the Simplon-Orient-Express.

## And Here the Story Begins

II

I is another.

RIMBAUD

Looking as if they'd been cut out of yellow, gray, and pink blotting paper by an arts-and-crafts lady's delicate scissors and set, with the filigree exactness of a ship-in-a-bottle, into the dove-gray–green of the water and the misted sky, the crumbling façades of Venice's palaces slipped past him as he rode along the Canal Grande to the railway station. Mischievously it occurred to him that the foaming waves churning up from his boat's broadening wake were contributing to the destruction to which this most surreal of all stilt settlements had been doomed since the advent of motors in the world of the gondola and sedan chair. His leave-taking of Venice was caustic; to judge by the degree of his malice, he must be in very good shape indeed, he thought to himself. Linda and her journalists were probably right: He was a cynic.

The heat was oppressive, and even the headwind did nothing to alleviate it. The air of the lagoons struck him full in the face like a warm, damp rag. Beneath his light suit, he felt his shirt sticking to his skin. It was an iron rule (part of the consciously cultivated Wall Street image) never to permit himself the slightest trace of sartorial negligence—except on Long Island weekends, of course. Wearing a collar open or draping a jacket over a chair seemed to him like taking one step closer to the horrors of lavishly flowered Hawaiian shirts and Bermuda shorts such as

115

his pensioned American colleagues wore—or like relapsing into Near Eastern sloppiness, he realized ironically, into the housecoat frowsiness of his Armenian aunts, who had much in common with the lethargic Miami blissfulness of which New York Jews dreamed just as avidly as Denise.

He had known for some time that he, like all his contemporaries, lived schizophrenically, in his own case in two kinds of pride: on the one hand, that of an American conscious of his nation's world power, gladly leaving cultural matters to the arts journalists; on the other, in the much more militant pride of the vulnerable, culturally coddled European. On his trip around the world he had behaved with the self-assurance of one invested with unlimited possibilities. With his American passport and his various golden credit cards, he placed not only the weight of a great power but also the hopes of the century on the hotel reception desks. He glowed with the aura of a solvent currency, worldwide economic influence, progressive technology, top-performance organization, unshakable confidence in the future. But already in Asia this prestige had become suspect to him, and the closer he got to Europe the more he realized that he could never feel completely American, not in his soul of souls, that he'd always looked down, considerately but skeptically, on his fellow Americans and their naive, undaunted, trumpeting optimism, looked down from a covert, superior, secure position as a member of a sadder, older race. Now, however, sitting in the stern of the motorboat, an Anglo-Levantine in a typically all too correct summer suit, Panama hat resting on his knees, and two antediluvian leather valises beside him, about to embark on the most touristy of all tourist trips possible, he had to admit that contrary to appearances he matched the American passport in his pocket more than his unresolved European inner life.

The journey he was about to undertake was American to the core. The train he'd be boarding in a few minutes belonged in Disneyland. Venice belonged in Disneyland, was just as anachronistic, had the same fairy-tale remoteness as the imitation of

116

Sleeping Beauty's castle in Florida; and he himself in this suit, which might just as well have been that of a slave-owning southern gentleman before the Civil War, fitted in capitally with this Ur-American landscape, far better than if he'd been clad in a sarong, with a Havana cigar stuck in his face, beside an obese Denise resplendent in bra and butterfly sunglasses on the terrace of a concrete condominium somewhere in the Caribbean. *Real* America, he told himself, was not the actual present but the fantastic, the utopian, the unreal.

That was where he was off to: unreality, American style; a dream journey very much to the American taste. For one evening, one night, and one morning—until he got to London—he would step outside the here and now and also become totally fluent in space, on the move in the pseudo-reality of an artificially reproduced past. He would indulge in these pseudo-experiences even more enthusiastically than Denise did at the movies or while devouring serialized novels in her magazines, for he wasn't simply a spectator or reader but a participant. What had been retrieved from unreality took on a deceptive, superficial life-immediacy, just as the horror scenes one observes from a ghost train at a fairground are more immediate than the medieval masters' depictions of hell one admires at cult palaces dedicated to fine art. Thus were Europeans trapped in their "priceless" values; Americans, more up-to-date and free-living, knew instinctively that experience could be had best in the most trivial abstractions.

He found it easy to slip into the role of a protagonist of his own past. In his anachronistically elegant clothing and cultivated deportment, he really felt a sense of identity with the fifteen-year-old boy who'd boarded that other Orient-Express train in Constantsa in 1930, then as now class-consciously correct and old-fashioned in clothes suited to someone more mature. The boy was traveling to London for the first time entirely on his own and was not, as in all previous years, escorted to the station by half a dozen clucking aunts—either stupendously fat or bony as mules, all of them reeking of spices, with long black moustache-hairs sprouting from under their cucumber-shaped Armenian noses. Not to mention the procession of oversolicitous domestics right behind them, bearing plaid blankets, coats, bags, and hampers fitted with roast chicken, figs, baklava dripping with honey, and other goodies one could eat safely only in a bathtub. While the servants stowed his baggage in his compartment under the watchful eye of his other relatives, his father's eldest sister—leaning on a stick to help take the weight of her enormous body off her poor feet in their black felt slippers, by now quite flattened—took him by the hand and marched down the length of the train, car by car, compartment by compartment, recommending him to the care, love, and protection of each and every one of his fellow passengers, including the governess of a thirteen-year-old girl; the girl herself, a slip of a thing, eyed him with a look of contempt he could never forget.

But now, at the age of fifteen, he'd shaken off the vigilant procession at last, had outgrown his childhood days and that shaming solicitude. He was going it alone, like a man, determined to enjoy the dangers ahead to the full. He dismissed his chauffeur at the station with a patronizing nod and handed over his luggage to a porter all by himself. He gave his ticket to the conductor with the blasé expression of a seasoned globe-trotter who had no cause to be impressed by the prospect of a journey across the breadth of Europe in a luxury train. Yet his heart beat like a hammer and his veins bulged in expectation of the adventures awaiting him, adventures that were less events than moods—thanks to the "genteel way of life of a nobler existence": *Oh, m'étendre sur le pont d'un grand navire, en route vers l'Insulinde!* . . .

Later there really had been an incident or two now and then that might well be called adventures, as long as one wasn't too demanding about the category. The very first—the Big One— had an impact of traumatic force (but the thirteen-year-old girl, who only a few years previously had scorned him so witheringly, wasn't there to witness his triumph—or, thank God, his defeat!). Over the years, these trips with their attendant dramatic incidents became routine. Year in, year out, he traveled to school in England and back home for holidays near the Danube delta at the Black Sea; and the legendary train that traversed the then still vast and variegated continent from Tower Bridge to the Golden Horn became more and more banal for him, especially since the entire epoch was beginning to forfeit something of its magic. The stylized nonchalance of the species that had survived the Roaring Twenties were visibly fading. The era dominated by those masters in the art of living was hurriedly drawing to a close. Operettas had transposed the mythological denizens of the Great World farther and farther east, until at the beginning of the new century they'd come full circle and merged with those of the newly emergent Golden West—the Central European monarch's son met up with the American millionairess, the midwestern railroad magnate courted the heiress to a Balkan principality. By now they'd all become rose-scented old wives' tales, the lot of them. Only in kitsch films and junk novels did crowned heads still travel incognito, waltz-crazy Balkan princes or beguiling Lotharios still bump into the orphaned daughters of five-and-dime kings who had traded places with their chambermaids because they wanted to be loved for themselves and not for their money. No longer did clever, ambitious chicks from the sticks, sexy but still chaste, run into devastating self-made oil barons who saw through their schemes but went ahead and married them anyway.

The whole field of adventure had been if not narrowed down then transported to the realms of the bourgeois. Even in popular fiction, the Tsar's courier had long been supplanted by the sheriff in cowboy boots and Stetson; Sherlock Holmes had hung up his deerstalker. In the visibly threadbare saloon cars of the Orient-Express, it was the crummy little Hercule Poirot who minced in and unmasked the criminal among the miserable group of passengers—swindlers, fixers, grand Levantine families four generations strong, daughters of the petite bourgeoisie who'd strayed from the straight and narrow and decided to replenish the dwindling supply of cocottes in Bucharest's Athénée Palace Hotel. True to the law of entropy, a vestige of the train's fashionable prestige still attained, and lent the passengers who declassed it something of its old romantic aura. (Denise, for instance, half a century later, got more worked up about a murder committed coolly among the upper classes than one done dirtily below stairs; and most of her contemporaries would surely find a flirtation consummated on the Orient-Express much more exciting than a romp on the backseat of a Volkswagen.)

Strangely enough—paradoxically even, if one considered America's democratizing tendencies—the two worlds that had been as close as siblings in dream life, began then, in the late twenties, to draw apart. The hitherto so felicitous exchange of myths between the old and the new no longer functioned as it should. Garbo, it's true, bridged continents, but only in a Chopinesque minor key, which infected the fading banjo and saxophone strains of the Charleston bands and mildewed at the tunes to which only recently Josephine Baker had kicked up her heels in Paris as vitally as the Ziegfeld girls had in New York. The Jazz Age passed just as surely as the Belle Époque had. Europe was now resisting the once so cheerful surrender to youthful America—and vice versa. It was as if the old continent had nothing left to offer the new, now that an inflation not only of currencies but also of marriageable aristocrats had broken out. Hearst had imported more than enough Romanesque abbeys and Gothic banquet halls, stone for stone, and the Crash rocked America's equilibrium fearfully. The old lady Europe pouted and withdrew to her own redoubt, trying to solve the problems of the ominously dawning age of the masses in her own way, ideologically well founded but ignoring a number of realistic factors. The ocean Lindbergh had flown across less than a decade earlier, to the rejoicing of two continents, was again broad and deep, sundering the two hemispheres. In Europe one renounced history and fell back on mythology, while America began to dispense with myth and discovered her own history. Pearl Buck warned that the winds of change blew on the other side of the globe too, and in the upholstery of the Orient-Express (so expensively restored in the resurrected one), the mice began to gnaw.

A sight he would never forget—it had served as a sort of coup de grâce to the old style of traveling; it must have been about 1937—was that of a man, black-haired, beefy, and Mongolian, in shirtsleeves and collarless, the livid red spot of the collar stud standing out on his hairy throat like a birthmark, hanging out of his open compartment window in the Bucharest railway station biting off little chunks of ice from a huge block and spitting them into an ice pack to give to his wife, who was suffering from a headache. Later the couple was met in Vienna by a group of Russian-speaking functionaries. The woman, dark and heavy, might well have been one of his Armenian aunts. In 1942 he saw the man again in Washington: he was first counselor at the Russian embassy. He got to know the wife as well: she was fragile and vivacious, with beautiful red hair.

Rumor had it that after the war the Orient-Express, seedy and lice-ridden, rolled on for a few more years behind the Iron Curtain, then finally ground to a halt. And now with its resurrection the spirit of a lost epoch had to be revived; but how could it be more than a ghost? He supposed even that would be looked on as an adventure in these dream-addicted days.

THE ELEGANT CURVE described by his boat as it pulled into the wharf in front of the railway station pleased him, as indeed did all things executed in a workmanlike and competent manner. He tipped the pilot generously and observed out of the corner of his eye how the man's respectful farewell affected the porters who came up eagerly to meet him. The train was standing somewhat apart from the prosaic commuter trains on the other platforms, its navy-blue cars freshly varnished, its iron spokes gleaming. Above the mirror-glass of the windowpanes could be seen the massive brass words of the familiar title: COMPAGNIE INTERNATIONALE DES WAGONS-LITS. The emblem SIMPLON–ORIENT–EXPRESS, Japanese-severe in gold, shone from the middle of each car like the coats of arms on royal landaus.

A reception committee of sorts awaited him at the head of the platform. Behind an improvised lectern stood a rather pretty girl—an English au pair type, with winning breasts and an expert way of bashfully batting her eyelids. She checked off his name on a list. A manager dressed like a civil servant welcomed him in the name of the company, voice and gestures ministerially hushed. A conductor, looking like a senescent cadet in his natty uniform, took his ticket and passport; a sleeping-car steward with yet more braid on his sleeve materialized to direct him to his compartment and see to his luggage with the porter's aid. And although he told himself that this kind of service was only in keeping with the price of the ticket, after all, the ceremony struck him as exaggerated, like those in the pompous restaurants Denise adored being taken to. It was awkwardly staged and contrasted too sharply with the confused gray shabbiness of the rest of the station. It wasn't different from the old days in Constantsa. Then as now he'd felt like an over-made-up actor shooting location scenes who pretends not to notice that his movements are mechanical, his limbs paralyzed by the awareness that he's dismayed as much by the attention of gaping crowds as by the indifference of those who hurry by. He wished that Denise were with him (she'd have adored it), and fled to safety inside the perfectly refurbished luxury train.

The train had been incubating in the sun for hours. The compartment, paneled with precious woods, was oppressively cramped and hot as an oven. He opened his overnight case and set about installing himself, thinking that his quarters had the confined coziness of a ship's cabin; the protected feeling of a cave nest, almost womblike, reminded him nicely just how few fundamental accessories he needed around him. The ultimate, truly economic form of housing with an absolute minimum of requisites, he thought to himself, would be a coffin, a simple cotton shirt the sole personal effect—

Even so, he'd have been grateful if it had been less hot; his stringent upbringing notwithstanding, he found it almost insufferable. Maybe air conditioning wouldn't be such a bad idea?

He laid out his toilet articles, his robe, pajamas, the thriller, the blood pressure pills and sleeping pills. The pedantic exactness with which he executed these actions—which he'd repeated many thousands of times in his life, after all—made him aware he was growing old. To compare his ceremonious, long-winded fussiness today with the unhesitating impetuosity of his younger years was to read clearly what measure of indifference had developed in the span of fifty summers. On that first trip alone he hadn't stayed in the compartment for a minute, so eager had he been to get a look at his fellow passengers, his prospective partners in the great adventure life was about to give him.

In the days before his first solo trip, when he'd still been carefully guarded, it had seemed as if all the exciting preambles, the trysts, intrigues, and plots that of necessity preceded every adventure, not to mention the adventures themselves, were being played out behind his back, part of the grown-ups' conspiracy of hiding the world from children and adolescents. Now here they were, about to take place in front of his waking senses. Whatever was mysterious and dangerous about them would test his courage, his intellectual mettle, his resolution, and his fiery spirit of enterprise. What made his pulse beat faster than anything his fantasy could depict in the lurid colors of expectation, however, was the utmost sublimation of risk and heroism and conquest: he'd read penny-dreadfuls and A. O. Barnabooth's verses as well; it was his voice that mingled with the "hundred thousand voices in the concertina train," dominated them, got them to sing, and its promise was that the adventure he was hurrying toward would be not only the experience of the heroic epic but also its promulgation: poetry.

Although it was hardly cooler outside than in, he tried to

open his window. The inscription on the little brass plate was as familiar as a childhood rhyme: *Ne pas se pencher au dehors! Do not lean out! È pericoloso sporgersi! Nicht aus dem Fenster lehnen!* He saw his aunt's richly ringed finger raised warningly. The warning was superfluous here, however; the window was screwed shut. Perhaps the company feared not so much the incaution of its own clients as the possibility that the rabble of normal passengers on other lines might attack the train's aesthetic integrity by hurling an empty beer can or a half-eaten hamburger through an open window. These days any form of privilege was so provocative that it had to be locked up.

There was no sign of any fellow travelers. The platform was empty too. Either he was the sole passenger or the others were sweating submissively in their compartments, perhaps beginning to dress for dinner; this was part of the planned gaiety after all, "formal dinner," with piano accompaniment—Blue Danube waltzes, no doubt. He decided to find out whether one could get a drink in the saloon car; he opened his door and stepped into the corridor. A steward quickly approached, a young man with protruding ears and a bony red nose set in a girlish pink face. According to the brochure, surviving members of the original Orient-Express staff had all been rehired; by his reckoning, these stalwarts would have to be at least eighty years old.

"Which route were you on before 1937?" he asked the lad jovially. "On the Bucharest–Budapest line, or on this one, Belgrade and Sofia, hmmm?"

"I was born in 1958," came the steward's stoical reply.

"I know, my son, I know," he said. His own son, had he ever had one, would have been ten years older than this kid. As he passed he patted the young man's thin arm in its wide uniform sleeve. Now he'll probably think I'm gay, he thought to himself glumly, though perfect service should also cater to such predilections in the clientele. He resisted the urge to tip the boy in advance; in bygone days, when he'd traveled alone for the first time, he'd done this with grand nonchalance, as a worldly uncle in Istanbul, a carpet dealer by trade, had advised him to.

The three cars he had to walk through to reach the saloon car were deserted, the doors to the compartments shut tight, no one in the corridor either. The heat was unbearable for normal mortals. In Braila, where he was born and grew up, it could get hot like this, and it wasn't much cooler on the estate in the Dobrudja, where he spent his holidays except on those occasions when the family went to Techirghiol, on the Black Sea. It was there that Kitty had first seen water buffaloes working in the fields. Just for fun people had taught one of the beasts to smoke; all the laborers received some tobacco as part of their pay, and laughingly they'd roll a cigarette and stick it in the buffalo's snout. A dark brown streak, glistening like the bowl of a well-puffed meerschaum, was burned into the moist reptilian skin of the animal's thick, pouting, gray-violet-pink lips. But the buffalo had long since become insensitive to the glow, was instead addicted, and refused to work if it didn't get the smoldering joystick. The smoke would come streaming from his nostrils in two silent blue fanfare blasts so that he looked like one of the bulls of Colchis with which Jason had done his plowing. . . .

What a shame I have no son to tell that story to, he thought to himself, as he pressed against the wall while a porter approached with several bulky suitcases. The door to the compartment for which these new valises were destined stood open. In the sharp, freshly varnished, hazelnut-brown paneling he caught sight of the intarsia whose photograph had so radically transported him into the past when he read the brochure. How was it possible that he hadn't noticed this motif in his own compartment? Perhaps he'd been taken up with the present, the desire to get installed as quickly as possible, and then cross swords with the new environment . . . and so on.

But no, that had been the case fifty years before, and it was a pretty deception to imagine he could mistake then for today. He was traveling on two parallel lines, so to speak, on this Disneyland choo-choo, in two adjacent, separate realities that took turns pursuing one another: the one ahead looking back, the other falling ever farther behind with its eyes facing the front. The actual present lay somewhere in between, like a kind of relay station, a field of awareness on which the questing contacts met.

He considered whether this put him at an advantage or a disadvantage vis-à-vis the other passengers, and if so, how great; he put the same question to himself almost daily in New York with regard to his American compatriots. Compared with him they had few historical reference points for the dream mutation of existence, and he could never decide whether the Old World's spiritual ballast and attendant lack of illusion made him safer than they were—on this tightrope walk with no safety net—or whether their naiveté increased their somnambulant security. Here, anyway, he was both European and American, and both to such a high degree of awareness that he was floundering in unreality.

The porter finished stowing the bags and now turned mistakenly to him for a tip. Before he could point out to the good man that he merely happened to be standing there, a voice sounded from the platform: *"No, prego, sono io!"*

The man speaking these words with a jagged German accent seemed familiar. Then in a flash he knew who it was, as the component parts of the image came into focus: the man's sharp club tie, the idiot son at his side with heaven's innocence shining from his eyes, and behind, the pluckily suffering, sportily optimistic wife and mother.

He avoided their brightly flaring eyes and shy smiles of recognition. Correctly and stiffly, he held back and waited until the Germans were installed in their compartment, then proceeded through the concertina-bellows to the saloon car. Here too, instead of a veteran, there was a young man in a white jacket getting the bar ready to receive the first guests. In the mythology of his generation, the bartender was a significant figure: companion and comforter, father confessor, fount of worldly wisdom and of potions to restore body and soul. It was almost shocking to encounter a beardless milksop one could hardly credit with knowing any drinks the fraternity of travelers might be partial to, let alone their spiritual needs. But he did know what a gin and tonic was, after all, and didn't make it too diluted either, so that enough remained from the little tonic bottle to provide, with another shot of gin, a second.

With the fourth drink the train was suddenly in motion. As they slid out of the station into the hazy late afternoon, he mused about the ancient Greeks' attributing to their gods that same sightless, non-blinking, all-seeing glance with which the idiot child had come lumbering into the car on his mother's hand. What devilish logic that this dumb child of God was also on the train!

Soon, toward Mestre, nothing was left of Venice but muddy lagoon water to the left and right of the rail causeway. What followed next was Americanik: the world as a construction site, nature as a ball park for unrelenting aggression, hybrid growth, sand pits and scrap heaps like a belt of mange ringing the metal-choked, metastasized sprawling hearts of the cities. The marrow-chilling emptiness of suburban playgrounds, iron bars, weedy chamomile between rust and mortar, the hard deserted sky of the industrial wasteland. For a moment he was stricken with homesickness for the breadth of America: that's where this violated landscape belonged; there progress would have been synonymous with ravishment. Here it was nothing but destruction. The cultural landscape of Europe was a garden, not the construction site of a world about to be vanquished.

He thought of his Romanian homeland and the peasants who carefully and modestly tended it; their primeval dark eyes as they followed the progress through their fields of the conceited, spit-and-polish navy-blue-lacquered train with its golden letters and reflecting windows. He thought of the eyes of the poorly clothed children his own age in the Constantsa railway station who'd watched as he was bundled into a train like this one by his aunts, nurses, and servants; the way they'd gaped at his dark blue blazer with maroon piping and the gold-embroidered school badge (the same as the one painted on the side of the cars?); the way they'd sniggered at his round school cap with its narrow peak, his knee-high socks, and his gloves—Little Lord Fauntleroy from Braila near the mosquito-veiled Danube delta on the Black Sea . . . the way the half-starved horses stood in their harnesses in front of the railway station and even bonier dogs dodged scruffy porters in military caps. He, on the other hand, had arrived in a Chrysler and the chauffeur had walked behind him carrying his duster: mother's boy, half-English, filthy rich Armenian father, importer of God knows what (Anatolian hazelnuts, Siberian silver foxes, Italian speedboat motors, and Czech cannons), "a boy with ready money," as the Romanian vernacular put it. . . . Out in the harbor a white passenger ship, luxury class, had lain at anchor, pausing on a Mediterranean cruise to the Golden Horn via the Crimea. The snotty-nosed kids in the station with their blank, staring eyes probably thought he had come from it. Well, let them think it; one day soon—really soon!—he'd sail through the great blue beyond on a ship like that, off to the shores of his reverie, and he'd leave them behind to dream a vicarious dream, now that they'd seen him. . . .

If it had been his intention to pursue what he'd lost, then he was traveling in the wrong direction. The no-more land of his innocence was in the East, there where his longing for the West had been born, not in the towns and provinces of the West itself, which meanwhile had become as bastardized American as he himself had; for just this reason he wanted nothing more to do with it. He preferred to remain displaced, since he was now even less at home in the Eastern half, and over there in America no better than a refugee. He'd written off so-called Western Europe too. Nothing made him squirm more than this hodge-podge of nations, this everybody's and no-man's land desperately concerned with its various little palettes of traditional colors while simultaneously striving for unity; this culture-saturated, culture-fatigued secondhand American province, laughable in the zeal of its imitation, tragic in the misunderstanding of what it imitated.

If there was anything left at all of his old Europe, then it was in the East, lost for him and his kind forever. Beyond the ideologies, beyond the murderously close-guarded boundaries, a trace of it was still left—not in the waltz-happy style of the Balkan operetta but in the secretly nurtured continuing European dream of itself. The land there was no longer a garden but a rubble-littered construction site of a future for which generations were prepared to trade the present, even if by doing so they ran the risk of having no future at all. There, in any case, the inmates dreamed of a Europe to which they'd once belonged and of which they still believed themselves to be a part, culturally at least. True, he was going in the wrong direction, but he should have thanked the Lord that the Disneyland choo-choo wasn't pulling out of Venice and heading east. For should they really get around to running the perfect toy train on all its old routes, with its gold emblems and precious wood inlays, crystal carafes, silver champagne buckets, cocktail hours with piano accompaniment, and luxury-class travel groups from Texas lounging behind the brass doorknobs; should this fake *train de luxe* indeed once more cross Europe Centrale to the Golden Horn, gently shaking its tourists *aux miraculeux bruits et vibrantes voix des chanterelles* and being pulled like the wind by *locomotives hautes et minces à la respiration légère et facile,* as Larbaud had sung the story, through the *solitudes montagnardes de la Serbie* or the melancholia of the Tisza River plain and *à travers la Bulgarie pleine de roses* or on to the black forests of the Carpathians; then it would be curtains for old Europe. Two different kinds of barbarism would have joined hands. Rat-catching sponsored by free enterprise together with the state machine would round up the rats and drive them along the sewers of their common interests. The people of shepherds *vêtus de peaux de mouton crues et sales aux pieds de groupes de grands arbres pareil à des collines* would be engaged by ministries of tourism and decked out in costumes borrowed from the state opera; tourist trains full of gum-chewing real and pseudo-Americans and their buddies from functionary circles in the East would join up the parts of Europe again; the import-export trade would run full blast; Hollywood cultural leisure-time video programming would run simultaneously too; and no catacomb communities would busy themselves learning poems by heart since the printing of these would be forbidden, no one would long to read uncensored editions of the pre-Hegelians.

Presumably he himself would be in there making money with the best of them. He hoped he could save his cynicism until he came home. He made up his mind to shock Linda's journalists once he'd gotten through the nonsense of his journey and returned to the weekends in the pioneer house on Long Island (and to the twilight hours in Denise's damask tent—there were television shows that made visits to out-of-town movie houses superfluous). He brooded about a tirade on the virtues of suppressing the spirit. He had fun visualizing the paralyzing effect this monologue might have; it could peak with the aphorism: "In order to keep the spirit alive, it must be forbidden." It surely would give protectors of liberal thought a moment's pause.

The saloon car began filling up. The pianist started his tinkling with "C'est Si Bon." He ordered another gin and tonic, his third. But it was really his fifth and would soon, with a further shot of gin and the rest of the tonic, be the sixth. He wouldn't get drunk, though. Now, in the evening of his life, he was used to hard liquor, regularly had his two or three martinis before meals (not to mention Denise's unspeakable concoctions) and his whiskey afterward, bravely and resolutely, like most of those who in fact do not care greatly for alcohol and would be happier with raspberry juice.

It had been at the bar of the Orient-Express that he had choked down his very first whiskey. He'd ordered it because an elegant woman sat beside him, observing him, and he would rather have been swallowed up by quicksand than drink something more innocent. Under her ironically glinting eyes, he'd gulped the whiskey down and ordered a second.

Half a century had elapsed since then. Even his delicate stomach had submitted to discipline, and his liver was intact, so far as the Mayo checkups could be trusted. At one point he had claimed that he owed his capacity for drink to his Anglo-Saxon half, that blond core within his darkly fuzzed Levantine husk, which as he aged covered over the delicate features of the Oriental mother's boy with something of the real legacy of the distaff side of his family—a line of robust London butchers.

He was too well formed, had too much natural pride, too much healthy self-respect to be ashamed of this side of his origins. After all, the Armenian side was no more aristocratic. His father would have treated a good butcher with the same courteous appreciation as a high-ranking minister of state, and with the same sharp-eyed appraisal and the same sympathetic acceptance of human frailty; in the best Armenian tradition, he revered his father above all else and took his conduct in every respect and under all possible circumstances as his paradigm (including, of course, his orneriness in business).

His schoolmates' mockery, when they found out that his English origins could be traced to a butcher's shop in Chelsea, only strengthened his pride, made him harder, more alert and composed, as any endured pain will do. For a pain it had been true enough, the painful loss of a magical illusion. He'd been sent to his school near London as "an Englishwoman's son"; in Braila— and even in Bucharest—that had meant a guarantee of privileges reserved for the very highest ranks in the social hierarchy, and in truth the aura of a most refined and costly education accompanied him all his life.

He'd been conscious of it from the beginning, and meeting his English relatives enhanced this feeling of distinction. Nothing in London thrilled him like the pink and red profusion of masterfully cut, beautifully arranged meat in the windows and display counters of his grandfather and uncles' establishment. He gazed forever at the rows of lamb chops, mustered like guardsmen in perfect straight rows with coquettishly appetizing paper frills at the tips of the bones. He loved the powerfully marbled steaks, the strings of sausages, the pale calves' and naked pink pigs' heads with serrated lemon-halves stuck in their snouts, the kidneys, which reminded him of rare stones, the dark livers set out on vine and laurel leaves, and—at the pinnacle of this virtuosity—the sculpted Britannia in the center, molded of snow-white lard, lions at her feet, and cut from colored paper and stuck to her shield, the blue field crossed fourfold with red and white, the banner under which Nelson at Trafalgar had fired the salute that signaled the founding of an empire. These seemed more beautiful to him than Marble Arch, more edifying than St. James's and the Guardsmen in their towering busbies, more artistic than the firefly-winged "Eros" in Piccadilly Circus. It was the essence of England. Later, when he heard of the War of the Roses, he involuntarily associated it with the vision of meat and fat and strong ale in pewter mugs that shone dully like the breastplates and helmets of the soldiers.

He loved his massive grandfather and his mother's freckled brothers, gazed in awe at their bare, powerful forearms covered in red fluff, gamely attempted to understand their cockney jokes, and in his occasional dealings with girls tried to imitate the frank and charming gallantry they accorded their female customers. He was deeply inspired, to the marrow of his bones, by Albion's phlegmatic existential certainty—nicely settled on a foundation of imperial self-confidence—when they laid aside their blood-stained aprons and, checked caps on their wiry heads and but-tonholes on their checked vests fairly splitting from the thrust of their swelling breasts, took him by the hand and brought him to "the dogs," the greyhound races, and afterward to the deafening conviviality of their local pub, where they made no secret of their prosperity.

When the unrestrained mockery of his schoolmates suggested

that all this was the last word in vulgarity, an occasion for shame and repression rather than pride, he angrily resisted their words and dealt a crushing defeat to their own wretched vulgarity. He felt his identity germinating within himself for the first time. But now, fifty years later, his enthusiasm for Britannia was gone for good. He saw his motherland with critically open eyes, although he didn't reject what he had hitherto cherished and what had nourished his self-confidence, and remained loyal to the arrogant assurance that he was "an Englishwoman's son." That his eyes had been opened to his mother's social station only set the record straight and revealed ever more clearly the intricate connection between things; it helped him take his first step from the domain of fiction into reality, and ultimately he was grateful to his schoolmates' class snobbery for this. If, in his soul, the wish to be one of the blond ones of the world remained alive, this was woven from the purest and tenderest dimension of childhood itself, its dreams, desires, visions. Even today, whenever he thought or spoke the word "blond," the deep soulfulness of his early life rang in the sound of it. His mother had been blonde. Kitty, his first love, had been blonde. Being blond belonged to the mythology of the age. Associatively, he believed that the brief years of his youth before the Great War, which buried them, had been as blond as Edward Albert David, Prince of Wales (later, in his dried-fruit stage, so to speak, the Duke of Windsor).

The elegant woman who had watched him choke down his first whiskey had been similar in type, come to think of it, to Wallis Simpson. (And the glance of the girl whose governess had been asked to keep an eye on him still smoldered in him fiercely.) Who could say how many things in his life might have turned out differently without the searching glance of that bewitching woman, indolently smoking from a foot-long cigarette holder, as he, for the first time in his life, sat on the barstool dangling his legs. . . .

In the fashion of the period, she wore a small turban of silver-gray silk, beneath which diamond earrings sparkled on both sides. He too had dressed for dinner, black tie, his first dinner jacket. He was not entirely at ease. At that time he was in the habit of looking rather often in his mirror, timidly hoping that behind what his Armenian aunts tenderly called their Fayoum, the almond-eyed Oriental oval of his boyish face, he would catch sight of the golden hair and peaches-and-cream freshness of the Prince of Wales, whom every young man in Europe thought of as the quintessence of elegance and good breeding. And although his own bow tie stood as immaculately above the points of his starched collar as did that of His Royal Highness Prince Edward Albert David, and his aunts had assured him at a previous rehearsal that his finely chiseled, darkly shaded adolescent face (reminiscent of late Upper Egyptian death masks) bore no direct resemblance to that of the pretender to the British throne (it would soon evince strong memories of the young Proust), he felt his evening attire was a presumption to which he had no right, and he wore it with little self-assurance.

The turbaned woman at his side, without taking her eyes from him, released her blue cigarette smoke from her nostrils in two soundless gusts. He was reminded of the Dobrudja buffalo, and this disgusted him. But then, just as he was ordering his whiskey and soda, she exchanged a glance with the bartender. To him it had seemed like a verdict, a matchlessly eloquent, unmistakable signal of contempt. He couldn't let it pass.

Later her mouth had tasted of cigarette smoke, had been wet and warm and violent, like the lips of a buffalo. . . .

THE TRAIN was moving very fast now; they must be near Verona and would soon come to Lake Garda, then Brescia. The saloon car filled up. Clearly there were more passengers than he'd thought there would be. They were English, mainly; worthy, affluent people, an insignificant bunch. How differently he might have experienced his performance today as an old-hand traveler if on his first trip alone he'd been able to assemble banal

134

biographies out of tiny external signs, so cold-bloodedly, as he could today! Certainly he would have deprived himself of a great deal of poetry; but in his adolescent respect for all things adult, he had transmuted every commercial traveler into a dispossessed aristocrat and every dental assistant into a duchess or *grande cocotte.*

To compensate for his lost illusions, he now proceeded to muster the people grouped around him with the eyes of a detective in a mystery story, picking out from the more or less ordinary types those most capable of murder, espionage, or jewel theft. This much the Orient-Express owed its reputation.

But the lineup was disappointing. Nothing pointed to the presence of even a potential con man. But then, was it still possible to be a con man nowadays? Yet another topic to entertain Linda's journalists with! In this age of advertising, where legions of "honest" copywriters called on heaven itself to witness that their products made things whiter than white, striving to rise above one's class had become an ethical imperative in one half of the globe, while in the other the proletariat had officially declared itself to be the highest, most privileged class; in a world living dangerously beyond its means, the con man's trade was robbed of its premise. Manolesco would have gone on the dole, or some ingenious person would have hired him as a floorwalker at Cartier's. . . .

The people sitting at the little tables here, in the flawless reconstruction of the piquant atmosphere of Decobra's novels, were exemplary citizens, pater- or materfamilias with dependable incomes and principles and healthy open minds for hobbies and pastimes, amenable (over and above gold and greyhound racing) to dream trips like this one. These sturdy men in their ready-made blazers and mass-produced shoes, well-nourished gents with open faces kept honest by the limitations imposed by a wealth of solid technical knowledge, together with the strapping fecund females at their sides, might one and all have been his own blood relatives; sons and daughters, grandchildren and great-grandchildren of butchers' families from Chelsea or Hampstead, Knightsbridge or Pimlico—but poorer for the loss of Britain's Imperium, and thus no better than watered-down Americans either.

There were a few of the real McCoy, sons and daughters of the New World, aboard the resurrected Orient-Express; one of them sat down next to him at the bar, talking to a group of his kind. The woman he appeared with—hard as nails and piercingly lovely, with a haze of something Asiatic about her—joined a group of other executive spouses in the background for a chat. The United States was sartorially represented by synthetic suits that could be washed and dried in the twinkling of an eye, skimpy pantlegs revealing white-socked ankles and disconcertingly large rubber-soled shoes. Unlike the British men, whose wiglike edifices of curls cascaded over their earlobes, full-blooded American men had their scalps shorn almost clean, especially above the ears, and they shone pinkly clean-shaven at the neck. Bulbous posterior muscles called to mind college football and heroic deeds in jungle warfare.

Only one couple, beyond their middle years and quietly speaking French with one another, recalled the standards of the old days; well-dressed cultivated Jews of the intransigent kind, he guessed, ever more refined and sensitive in the face of general brutalization. Presumably they had emigrated from Germany or Austria in time, resettled in some sanctuary for the relics of European civilization—Switzerland or Holland. They too looked around as if sensing the absence of something that had been promised in the brochure. They seemed straight from Central Casting, but surely this notion did not occur to them.

He was not in the habit of discussing other people (unlike Denise, for instance, who was always telling him stories about her customers and other people he'd never clapped eyes on), but if there had been a barman of the old school here, he might well have exchanged a few words with him apropos of his fellow travelers. Viz., it seemed obvious that the gentle, cultured couple were the only ones so far traveling privately for their own pleasure—probably to commemorate some precious anniversary or other, the date of a blissful honeymoon in Venice perhaps. All the others were on an expense account, and at the expense not of their own firms but of some larger sponsor. From various remarks he ascertained that they had something to do with the Orient-Express company and were traveling at its invitation.

So then, this was like the rest of the antiques trade: here too the overwhelming majority of buyers were from the same business, dealers and sellers interested in keeping goods in circulation, with only the offal on the market and actually sold to naive customers, while the more exquisite items went from dealer to dealer at spiraling prices. So in the travel industry as well, he presumed, especially in the luxury branch, the most interested customers were other travel industry representatives, seeking a connection with some profitable project in order to franchise it even more profitably. Physicians might well gain deeper insight into the phenomenon of metastasis by examining this circumstance.

He took a swig of his gin and tonic and was relieved to note that there was little risk of his being surrounded by his financial compatriots, as there had been at the hotel swimming pool. The difference between him and these American tribes was subtle, though, for in one tax-favored way or another they all worshipped the same god.

These reflections were interrupted by the arrival of a family whose ghostlike quality conjured up the romantic old "grand world cruise" one last time. The man, who entered first, held open the folding door to the bellowslike platform between the two cars for the woman behind him; he was well into his seventies and English to a point of caricature—the stiffly twirled white moustache of a picture-book colonel under an avian nose, the eagle eye adorned by a gleaming monocle, the drooping bloodhound dewlaps of his cheeks merging into a scrawny neck with a sharply jutting, commander's Adam's apple. About his shoulders sagged the elephant hunter's faded bush shirt and safari vest; about his storklike legs, sun-bleached, reed-colored linen pants; his feet were stuck into colorless, misshapen desert boots, and he limped extravagantly on what seemed to be a poorly fitting artificial limb, supporting himself on a stick. The arm that stretched naked from the short sleeve of his shirt to hold open the door and enable his lady to step through was sinew and bone contained in an abundance of skin, like that of a very old woman.

Then the wife. She was ancient too, this lady for whom he made way with such antiquated chivalry. The sparse, curly, close-cropped hair on her head was not white but parchment-yellow, tinted slightly pink by the skin of her scalp shimmering through. Her face too drooped in folds, as though she'd hung it out to dry, and her evil little watery blue eyes glittered as piercingly as the diamond clasp of her pearl necklace, whose thick strands piled one on the other separated like a precious dog collar her squat pug head from her massive torso. Over an evening gown decorated with flowers of a size usually reserved for chintz sofas she wore a faded Afghan wrap of multicolored moiré silk; it must have already had a brittle patina in the days of King Amanullah; from beneath the hem of her ankle-length skirt peeped a pair of well-worn tennis shoes. The majestic assurance of her entrance made it clear that it had been her habit to present herself to her surroundings in this same outfit for three-quarters of a century, day in and day out, in bush camps or the yurts of nomadic tribesmen, in the lounges of Raj polo clubs or the clay huts of Borneo's dripping jungle, in the mess rooms of Red Cross nursing contingents in Flanders or behind the lines at El Alamein, in sandstorms and tropical downpours, shaken by malarial fever and wracked by dysentery cramps, sober, brusque, just, and imperious. She was a monument from a great epoch, a pillar that had managed to remain upright among the ruins of Albion.

But it was the son of this remarkable couple, following closely on his parents' heels, who arrested his interest most particularly. He was some fifty years of age; the hair at each of his temples, meticulously combed into a sort of curlicue, was snowy gray, the scrupulously shaven face as informative as a closed book. He had the immediate elegance of a Rolls-Royce salesman, and everything about him observed the same standards of quality. One got a whiff of his Floris eau de toilette without its being obtrusive; his hair, chestnut brown except for the snow at the temples, shone from the brisk strokes of Asprey brushes; his chalk-striped suit betrayed the master hand of Huntsman; beneath it, snow-white Turnbull & Asser linen was discreetly visible; his shoes came from the workshop of Lobb. He was just as much a walking testimonial for trademarked consumer articles as any wearer of becrocodiled polo shirts, Levi's jeans, or Adidas shoes; but his status symbols were more esoteric, legible only to the eyes of richer initiates.

And the initiate was of course aware of the magic of the decoded message. The Rolls-Royce salesman's sumptuous elegance could not conceal the ulcer-inducing dependency on everything that was so suffocatingly limiting about the bourgeois world—its libidinal repression and existential angst, its slavish obedience to superiors and its tormenting, halfhearted, yet stubborn quest for God. It was elevating to see the whole ensemble in all its perfection and banality standing there, to see a man in an existential blind alley, caught like a mouse in the trap of his own programming, convinced that precisely this was the proof of his inhabiting a supreme plane of existence.

This type of neurotic arrogance had inflicted many wounds on the self-respect of a half-Armenian butcher's grandson in his youth. But seeing this pathetic last case was not a balm that could heal his deep life-sadness which now, fifty years later, was tapering off into a fundamental sense of the mutability of things, both soothing and paralyzing—as though growing older had the same effect as poppies. So he looked without animosity on the fourth of the picture-book British, a perfect replica of one of his schoolmate tormentors. The young man made him remember how he had boarded the old Orient-Express in London with mixed feelings: on the one hand, grumpy at having to leave the civilized Western world (and then later the joys of the Sphinx in Paris) for the heavy, oven-warm spice-laden scents at home in Braila and the mud-crusted work-buffaloes of the Dobrudja; on the other, very glad in his secret heart to get away from the humiliations and humilities, like an exiled prince who is liberated and returns to his rightful kingdom, where, after a long period of spiky incognito, exquisite honors await him.

The young man who followed the other three Britons was clearly the son of the Rolls-Royce salesman and grandson of the white hunter and memsahib; he had unmistakably taken after Grandmama. Her pug face had not become ennobled in his, but because of long-skull genes somewhere, better contours had come about: the nose was sharper, finer, the cheekbones more delicate, the eyes bigger, more open. The boy was not smaller, but rather more compact than his father; a well-worn tweed jacket and bleached jeans (in which the anatomy of his pelvis and sex, his muscular hiker's thighs and his knees showed through as with a sodden shroud) clothed a turgid, brutal physicality. His blond hair was cropped short; his walk on scuffed boxer's bootlets was firm and elastic; his chin, above a short neck in an open collar, though not prominent, was thrust forward; and his glance was fixed straight ahead. Well, the glance betrayed the habit of consuming medium-strong dope. It was the opposite of the listening, distant look in the eyes of the German idiot child, and yet the rigidity of the pupils, nailed in the watery blue of the irises, was aimed straight at the undertow of the great world void. The breadth of the lost Empire was held there as firmly as in the wafting melancholy of a Beatles song.

The quartet moved through the saloon car looking neither right nor left, occasionally shaken off balance by the movement of the train as it thundered across points, obliged to adopt the swerving serpentine gait of drunkards or sufferers from tabes. In this fashion they proceeded to the other end of the car and then out again; once more the ancient elephant hunter held the door open for the pillar of the Imperium, once more son and grandson followed, the one with the immaculateness of a Guard officer, the other with the somnambule indifference of the slightly but permanently high. They all left behind them an unreality, the impression of an apparition.

In the meantime the voice of the American beside him at the bar diverted his attention. He listened. The man was giving a little improvised lecture to a small circle of passengers. Science today, he argued, opened up possibilities that were not yet fully comprehended, not by a long haul, let alone exploited. Effortlessly, by linking certain brain cells with computers, we can now take in and store up the material knowledge of entire disciplines, of archaeology say, Sinology, astronomy, metallurgy, paleontology, whatever we like; not only in order to have it at our disposal when we want it but also in order to profit from the edifying influence that all knowledge exercises on the knower. At the tips of our fingers, we have, he imagined, the ability to probe the vast immensities of space from satellites, using lasers and various kinds of rays—experiencing the heavenly bodies physically and, with them and among them, setting up an almost erotic connection, so to speak. In short: We are not yet truly at home in the present. People today are lamely hobbling along, way behind the age they live in. . . .

The good soul from Texas was talking himself into a passion. With the irritating monotony of his voice somewhere between the bellow of a rutting stag and the entreaty of a lay evangelist, he expounded on the notion of a man capable of utilizing to the full the potentialities of today's technology: a spider, as it were, hanging in the center of the cosmos, suspended in the web of its three-, four-, or five-dimensional connections. . . .

Then a razor-sharp "Darling!" stopped him dead in his tracks with his mouth hanging open. His Eurasian wife was calling him to order: he should be so good as to stop blathering and come change for dinner. It was a scandal, she added to his circle of thwarted listeners as they departed, that on this so-called luxury train there were no showers. Her visionary spouse obediently toddled after her.

The incident was funny, and involuntarily he raised his eyes, which he'd directed downward during the oratory, and met the glance of a woman on the barstool beside his own. When had she arrived? Later he said to himself that he must indeed have registered her arrival but determined that close examination would not pay off. On any other occasion she would have slipped to the peripheral zones of his attention; at this moment, however, their mutual understanding was perfect.

Both smiled as they watched the future-man go off. He invested his smile with a deeper warmth, expressing thus his gratitude for this spontaneous rapport. Then he asked, "What language shall we speak?"

"English, French, Italian, Spanish, whatever you like," she replied. Her eyes were bright and hard, like the sparkling one-carat diamonds in her ears. But the smile stayed on her lips, somewhat mocking yet with no trap of temptation. The wrinkles around her eyes made it plain that she'd pluckily crossed the thirty mark. Her flaxen hair—lightened by bleach, he thought—curled in short, thick lamb's-wool ringlets; they looked firmer than Denise's wood-shaving curls, and must feel like the fur of a poodle, he imagined.

Her clothes were simple but not without a certain chic. The jade-green summer dress and light shoes on stockingless brown feet revealed good taste. But on her short-fingered, brutal hands there sparkled several rings of flawless one-carat diamonds: these were the jewels favored by resolute demimondaines as portable and quickly negotiable capital investments. Her smile told him that she was clever and had a sense of the absurd. The composure with which she had eased into the conversation was a sign of maturity, however attained.

She pleased him for the moment. Intuitively he recognized her. He knew he need fear neither Denise's irritating puerilities nor Linda's pseudo-intellectual embellished icy-coldness. Her bright eyes seemed to tell him that she intuitively knew him too. This encouraged him to imagine that earlier she had agreed with him about the picture-book Britons; and thus that she knew just what it had been about the Rolls-Royce salesman and his son that had opened the old wound in his injured self-respect and, with the rejoicing of the victorious, alleviated but not healed it; and also knew that this wound was but the smallest source of his melancholia. She knows about my Grail sufferings! shot through his head unreasonably. A thought exalted to the point of taste-lessness, but not irrelevant.

He resolved to store it for later reflection. For the moment, the woman was keeping him busy. "Your glass is empty," he said, continuing in English, as he believed it to be her mother tongue.

But when she answered without hesitation, "There was vodka in it," he heard the trace of an accent after all.

"Scandinavian?" he asked.

"Finnish," she replied.

He signaled to the young bartender that he should refill their glasses. The futurologist's audience had dispersed. They were alone at the little bar.

"Shall we continue the guessing game?" he asked. "What do you think I am?"

"Diplomat?" she asked in return.

"You are very clever, my child." He laughed, softly clinking his glass on hers. "I can't imagine a better way of reducing the full range of possibilities—Latin American gunrunner, Levantine middleman, California mafioso—to the common denominator of what one hopes is a respectable external appearance."

"I'm a tour manager for an international travel agency," she explained without pressing for a proper answer from him. "You develop an eye for these things."

143

Once again he smiled involuntarily; so he *had* assessed the composition of his traveling companions accurately. But his satisfaction at his own perspicacity was undermined by a deep sadness in realizing that the world loses its magic through a too perfect knowledge of its ways, and his smile took on a melancholy tinge. She was still regarding him with unswerving attention, and he fancied she knew the reason for his dejection. He felt that he owed her something.

"You are beautiful," he said.

"Are you sure you didn't forget your contact lenses?" she retorted; and when he said, "I don't wear them," she followed up with, "Then your mistake is excusable."

He said, "You know very well I'm not mistaken. When you look in the mirror you may find your nose is a trifle short and your mouth perhaps too large, or you'll see some other minor imperfection or the signs of fleeting youth and all that nonsense. But that has nothing to do with the beauty of a person who has thought of herself as someone agreeable—more agreeable than most anyone else around—always excepting of course such divinities as movie stars or champion athletes, Nobel Prize winners and the like—"

"And the younger sister, perhaps, who really was beautiful," she interrupted.

"If also stupider—"

"But which didn't stop you from thinking she was more beautiful, constantly measuring yourself against her and others who were all more agreeable, one way or another, so that in the end you were robbed of self-respect. Oh yes, later on you reconstruct it out of a mass of comparisons and details, but not enough for a successful delusion." She drained her glass with an experienced flick of the wrist and thrust it toward the youthful bartender.

"But enough to convince a few others of your agreeableness?" he concluded.

"Oh, dozens," she said laughing, "although there too the

feathers flew, didn't they? To make a long story short: I'm an old campaigner and therefore the perfect partner for you. *Skål!*" She clinked her refilled glass against his.

"*Skål,*" he answered, taken a little unawares. "Why don't we discuss the details over dinner?"

"With pleasure. I just have to go change out of this rag." She made a small gesture that circumscribed their surroundings in a vague and ironical manner: "We owe it to the *ambiente,* after all."

"Of course," he said. "It'll do me good to change into something else too."

And then, like someone lapsing into inattention as the pressure of great tension begins to slacken, he added, with astounding banality, "It's scandalous that there's no air conditioning on this train."

"Or showers!" She chortled. They laughed and parted to go to their respective cars, he to one behind the saloon car and she to one in front.

HE REFUSED to think about what he was letting himself in for. Dining together committed him to nothing for the time being. There was something fishy, though, about the glib way she'd taken charge of things. But he was no longer so young and foolish as to feel that this undermined his manly dignity.

At the age of fifteen, in 1930, he would have found it unbearable; but the woman in the pearl-gray silk turban had been clever enough to appear to be leaving the initiative to him. Today he knew that it must have entertained her to watch him going through his paces to reach a goal that merely corresponded to her preconceived intention. He saw her now before him, as though he'd just parted from her in the bar: She was sitting there on the barstool with her legs crossed—her legs had been the only part of her he'd seen with any precision as he approached with his head bowed; the rest of her was background, dimly perceived at the edge of his field of vision. But it was breathtaking background: the close-fitting dress of the same pearl-gray material clutching her trim body with its small breasts; stupendous brooch in the center of the turban vying for brilliance with the diamonds in her earlobes (what an amusing coincidence, those diamonds!), the sparkling clasps at each side of her plunging neckline, her throat and shoulders exposed, the naked upper arms, the vermilion gloves that covered her elbows. It was all in the fashion of the day and gave the inevitable *fatale* note.

Her dress, smoothed tightly over long thighs like a silken skin, ended just above the knee, so that her legs were displayed to full effect, gloriously slender, excitingly beautiful in silk stockings that gleamed like the slicks snails leave behind, legs the likes of which one saw in ads in glossy magazines, erotic fantasy-images that are permanently imprinted in the hearts of boys headed for manhood and that determine the course of life. Only when he'd clambered up onto his barstool (clumsily, he feared) did he see that the youthfulness of her legs contrasted markedly with her hard facial features and the crow's-feet around her eyes. Oddly, this did not repel him; on the contrary, he construed it as something maternal in her, a kind of guarantee that she would be fond and kind and let him have those legs as a plaything. He had had no idea, of course, how very much this wishful thinking corresponded to reality.

Even now he could no longer remember how he got into conversation with her. All that was still clear was the image of her arm, propped on its elbow, the hand moving a foot-long cigarette holder to her thickly painted lips. As he talked, she held it between her teeth and played with the mouthpiece with her tongue so that far out from her face the tip of the glowing cigarette danced in the air like a baton beating time to his words—an erotic secret language, he had a mind to believe, whose signals he dare not misconstrue.

Every so often the greasy red lascivious rolls of her lips would pucker around the mouthpiece as in a kiss and suck on it sensuously, only to open again, as her nostrils expelled the blue smoke through which she examined him with her bright ironic eyes as through a slowly dispersing veil—him, the lad in the all too new, all too perfect evening clothes, all too clearly his first; him, the young and fearless whiskey-drinker who could scarcely conceal his aversion to the awful fluid tasting of medicine; him, the fifteen-year-old libertine and seducer who hid his embarrassment under a torrent of fantastic anecdotes that swept him further and further away from any hope of saying something not too blatantly indicative of his real purpose.

Her maternal feelings must have been touched by his fatuous eagerness to play the young roué; she had to fall in love with the clumsiness with which he was trying to seduce a woman who was only too willing and, finally, with his desperation at the catastrophe in her bed. Even today he still shuddered to think of her rough-throated caresses.

NIGHT HAD FALLEN on the country they were passing through. The image of his compartment, pale and transparent, transfixed by the reflection of the little lamps in the interior, was imprinted on the windowpane; behind it dark shadows whooshed past and, behind them, orchestrated by the rise and fall of telegraph wires, flowed meadows and vineyards and Lombardy's hills; in the darkness beyond, the mountains of South Tyrol rose slowly into view.

In the old days it had been the forests of the Transylvanian Carpathians through which his glowworm train had twisted, along white-frothing streams tumbling between black mountains. To the lonely shepherds on the slopes, sitting with their shaggy sheepskins flung around their shoulders, their chins resting on hands clutching the ends of long hazel sticks, listening to the thunder of the wheels approaching and then dying away far off in the night landscape, the sudden sight and swift disappearance of the glittering column, slithering and twining through the loops and turns of the valleys, recalled the fire-spewing dragons of the fairy tales their womenfolk recited as they shucked corn down in the village. The smoke-tanned rooms of their mud huts, capped with mushroom-shaped thatched roofs, were gilded with the dust of the cobs; children with eyes like black cherries squatted sleepily, spellbound by the wonders they heard at their mothers' knees. The men smoked their pipes and spat into the fire; toothless grinning old men nodded their shrunken patriarchal heads with gleaming pates and cascades of silver hair at the sides.

This all belonged to his homeland, which he had insolently betrayed each time he rode out to the West in one of these fiery dragons—out to the world of a thousand and one excitements, cities with the magic sparkle of myriad light bulbs, nerve-racking rhythms switching them on and off, Bengal lights in the night sky flaring up and dying above a cacophony of vehicles and humans, the titillating twinkles ebbing to glowing patches through which the luminous strings of neon letters ran into the gaping cavern of the night's gloom, leaving behind an even blacker pit of darkness, the sputtering comets in their wake briefly illuminating passing car windows through which one caught a glimpse of a female eye glinting above the costly comfort of a turned-up fur-trimmed collar.

The far world of the West was a world of a future megalopolis. Its towers of high-rise lights soared heavenward, and between them express trains raced back and forth on the crazy-woven spider webs of tracks, assembly lines rolled, missiles shot hither and thither; and in this utopian world of "comfort and communication," a new, sport-trimmed, health-fed, functionally clothed, and scientifically directed humanity would be granted golden happiness forever.

For now it was a world of a chaotic, exciting, nocturnally brilliant present; Josephine Baker updated Mistinguett's ostrich-feather bustle with an arrangement of bananas about her loins, and they both sang songs of praise to the erect phallus of the Eiffel Tower; half of mankind danced in tails and tuxedos, silk gowns and diamond earrings to the velvet tones of saxophones and the enervating rhythms of banjos, and the other half marched through the streets announcing strikes; all of them swayed in delirium at the shrine of Mammon, thanks to whom this whole effervescent present was possible. Lost dreams . . .

The reflection of the lamps ricocheting on the crystal and silver in the dining car, where the waiters, the black butterflies of their bow ties contrasting sharply against the chalk-white front of their shirts, attended the first guests, was a transparent pictorial anticipation, a dreamy promise, of all the glowing, sparkling, glittering events, countless excitements and enticements this dream train was headed for. The discreet tinkling of the piano ("J'ai Deux Amours" then, "C'est Si Bon" now, with the inevitable Blue Danube waltz thrown in for good measure) enhanced the fashionable atmosphere like the musical accompaniment to a silent movie, holding its own against the monotonous thudding of the wheels on the iron rails, as they moved thunderously across points to another nowhere, bearing the dark-blue brass-bound blinking cars with their somnambulist cargo.

And he was fifteen years old.

Through the compartment window the restless black background of firs was as unfathomable as the mirrored surface of a wishing well. The fire dragon hurtled along, splaying branches this way and that; and he, standing there tying his tie and pretending to himself that he was gazing out into the night—the great, good night that rose to a spatter of stars each time an overlap of two mountains shook free and cleared the way—checked his reflection hanging in midair between the sharp black slopes, checked to see whether the sarcastic eyes of the thirteen-year-old girl might still mock his childish awkwardness, or whether in the meantime he'd acquired enough worldliness to stand the test of an adventure, to enslave to his will any woman the train might be carrying.

He'd had a lot of experience by now, after all. His love for his cousin Kitty had been great and pure, destined to last forever, but it had grown oppressive to the point of pain (the first stormy rattlings of the prison bars of ego, from which there was no escape), and this had led them not only to nirvana, to a world union of sweetly melting togetherness, but also, more intensely, to a much earthier experience. The Madonna image he'd fashioned of his first love couldn't obscure the sense that the budding young body he'd breathlessly pressed to his own wasn't *her* at all but a pledge, a hostage, to the ideal of *woman,* and that the fluffy, softly swollen double swelling above the warm moist slit between her smooth thighs, which he'd been allowed to touch, was not only the gateway to the ultimate paradise, the contented union with the other, but also the way to a finally accomplished, robust reality of life, to a final realization of manhood.

Only a few months later there was nothing left of the summer he and Kitty had spent in Braila and on the estate in the Dobrudja except a few poorly focused, unsteady, over- or underexposed snapshots with which memory is content to store important (and umpteen unimportant) moments in life: the pale freckles scattered over Kitty's little nose, the corn-colored hair at her temples; the bubbling liveliness with which she explored the unknown in this strange Oriental land, the shabby town, the lazy river with its boat traffic to the Black Sea, the steppes behind the mosquito-veiled lagoons; her being in love too, of course, her joy at his being the same; all sorts of climatic favors bestowed by their adolescent love—colorfully blazing sunsets that transformed the mist in which the contourless plain was lost into a blinding sheet of light, as if it were the end of the world; timid-blue twilights in which the croaking of multitudes of frogs in distant ponds clothed the tone and atmosphere with finely hammered silver; glass-clear full-moon nights, the sky devoid of stars and the land like a corpse in a coffin, zephyr breezes playing with a strand of its limp hair; the welcome solitude of a copse of trees in the middle of a vacant field, in whose mint-scented shade they threw themselves after a hard ride, hot, worked up, dazed, curious about each other; a tango playing on a gramophone, and them dancing cheek to cheek in a doorway between two rooms, one lit and the other dark, drawn to the dark one but not brave enough to leave the light . . .

And of course, the memory of painfully beautiful moments plagued him too, the moments when they were exhausted from kissing, emptied by unfulfilled desires and filled with guilty feelings about their passionate caresses; moments when they grasped each other's hands, turgid, and silently vowed eternal loyalty and devotion, each from the bottom of a thumping heart and despite the inner voice whispering at them, warning that fate had ordained something quite different for them.

And so he found out, without too much surprise, that the end of a love, even if at first it seemed as though one should pluck out one's bleeding heart along with the roots of that love, also brought delights of healing: an awakening from the madness, however marvelous it might have been; a freeing of the soul from all the weighty ethical and moral ballast that fiction had loaded onto love, from Chrétien de Troyes to Judith Krantz—in short, the refreshing sense that life could now continue, uncomplicated and brisk.

H E  W O U L D N ' T put on a dinner jacket and bow tie this time. His dark suit was festive enough for dinner with a casual partner whose compliance to subsequent sexual dalliance he need not doubt. The landscape in his window began to break up; the train was slowing gradually, pulling into the mangy outskirts of a town. He saw from the increasing ugliness of the houses, looming out of the darkness in an ever more cramped and grayly inhuman form, that it was in fact a big city. It must be Milan.

The usual scenes: the golden glow of the train windows sliding across the shadowy blank walls and falling away into the chasms of the streets in between; the floury light of an arc lamp glaring across a row of parked trucks; irregularly placed yellow window squares against the black of their framing walls; other, blind windows giving on to living-caves in which anonymous life was hidden away like unsolved murders; coal heaps, wooden fences; the light-rivers of streets heading to cold, distant sources of energy, coloring the roofs a fiery red; farther away, the crossword-puzzle lights of high rises; the night above heavily misty, close, with no future: over and over again the same old tired night after the same old futilely elapsed day. Exhausted humanity, life lived to the point of pointlessness, wretched mass pleasures here and there whipped into mass hysteria ready to perpetrate mass crime.

There was no doubt as to the outcome of the dinner he was about to have. He and the stranger would perform the act they'd been brought up to consider the ultimate, confirmative life-reality—the only thing a solitary creature is equipped to do that will combat the void of existence; the only justification of existence over and above the quest and intake of food, the digestion and expulsion of food; the most primeval of all motivations; the desperate expression of the tenacious collective will to survive; an act of procreation as a minimal contribution to the tremendous dam-building project erected against the inevitability of death. They would again be drawn into the most trivial of all mass activities, the most stupefying of all mass-experienced experiences, continuously experienced and executed by millions every fleeting second of every fleeting day, ending by the millions in the Black Nothing of desperation, even in the climactic delirium of love. . . .

The same activity he'd shared half a century before with the woman in the silver-gray turban. Now it was worse, a consummation all the more devoutly to be wished on account of his initial failure. He thought back on that moment with more than simply understanding forbearance. It put everything else he had ever experienced in the way of horror into the shade.

SHE'D BEEN FULLY PREPARED when she admitted him to her compartment. Beneath the transparent nightgown she was quite naked. But she'd kept her turban on, and he had a frightening vision of her being bald beneath it, or perhaps worse—scabies, or that scourge of promiscuity, syphilis (on which subject his aunts had often given him hell).

It was too late to back off now; it was the same as with the whiskey he had had to drink at the bar. Behind everything hovered the mocking smile of the thirteen-year-old girl of those four years before, and his unfulfilled dream of love with Kitty; the sarcastic challenge of the English schoolmates to whom he'd boasted about his prowess; the lessons and bragging of the stablehands in the Dobrudja, the obscenities of the Romanian guttersnipes in Braila; the secretly perused pornography and overheard scraps of adult conversation, things furtively viewed at the cinema; the dread of pubescent acne; the tormenting guilt about the vice of youth he'd practiced for years, which, it was said, could blind you . . .

He gathered up all his courage and ripped open her nightgown with a roughness he supposed to be the mark of a man of the world—and almost recoiled in horror at the sight of a great bush of jet-black pubic hair, crisp and taut and coarse as twists of horsehair peeping from the slit in a mattress, thick as the beard of a Greek seminarian. . . .

Of course there was no reason for it to have been blond. Blond was pure, was chaste, was heavenly. Black was seduction, lust, sin—and he'd neither expected nor wanted anything else here. Still, this coal-black wedge of satanic fur seemed like the funnel to damnation.

Yet he was brave, desperately determined. The gymnastics they performed on her very narrow bed as the train twisted through a notably tortuous stretch of the journey led to nothing; he couldn't generate any excitement over her body, although it was youthfully shapely. She seemed to him old like a gnome, and her ardor was repulsive; he reeled away from her painted death's-head and was queasily careful not to touch her turban for fear of revealing a final horror beneath it; shuddering, he avoided her man-eating kisses, the violence of her fumed and lipstick-smeared buffalo lips, the stench of alcohol on her breath. . . .

But he'd been too young to give up, and so the rout had been total.

A WEB OF RAILS weaving back and forth, from side to side, led to shunting yards. Freight trains waited in line like trails of night workers or rolled slowly along in endless chains of barrel-shaped tankers; or the rails brought them up to approaching columns of trucks, filled with dung-bespattered cattle behind trellised wooden walls, or packed with the multicolored metal, rubber, and gleaming paint of factory-new automobiles. This awoke in him the nightmare vision of ever more traffic, ever more roads choked with vehicles, like the twigs of a plant beset by lice. The darkness was pierced by hard points of light, and enormous water pumps loomed up like antediluvian mammals. Stiff signal posts suddenly let their arms drop commandingly to right angles as they closed one green dragon's eye and opened the other, red, gleaming like those of Orcus. And over everything rose Milan's cold glow, like the promise of a fairy-tale world or the threat of a great fire, into the mists of the starless heavens.

He pulled the shade down over the window with such vehemence that he frightened himself. He told himself that it was a protest against the ludicrous, banal feeling of guilt that crept up on him on such occasions now that Denise had woven herself into the tapestry of his existence (more than he liked to admit).

The train would stop in Milan and put its glittering contents on display—not accidentally, he presumed; the Orient-Express was its own best advertisement, announcing itself with its opulence, its passengers obligated to take part. This gave his trip a bitter aftertaste. Already in Venice he'd had the ineradicable impression that this perfectly produced, anachronistic luxury was a provocation, if not a total outrage. His picture of himself as a dandified, smarmy adolescent standing in his gold-buttoned navy-blue blazer on the scruffy railway platform in Braila among ragged porters and gray-faced railwaymen, loiterers and third-class passengers with their goats, hens, wives, and children—for him this image summoned up all the tumult of socialist polemics in the century. An epoch charged with class hatred pointed its accusing finger at the brass-and-blue railway cars. And he had to admit that contrary to his steadfastly held opinion and conviction, at one time the backbone of his self-assurance, this was a reason for secret shame and remorse.

The impulse to run and hide had deeper roots than these, however. Whether riches spelled guilt, whether luxury constituted an outrage were relatively trivial questions. He sensed that he'd let himself in for something that was beyond his control. This train, with its cargo of knaves in its precious wooden, sparkling copper-, bronze-, and brass-bound cars, careening through the night like a giant electric toy, did not ask to be taken seriously. Whoever rode on the dream vehicle participated in a put-up job, declared his belief—even if he did it with eyes wide shut—in the idea that the clock could be turned back and that one could travel again in an epoch of unburdened social conscience. Inside the train one might get dizzy from the mixture of Belle Époque decor and late-twentieth-century manager faces, of Art Deco and Sunday-best well-insured kitchen coziness. But one need only look out of the window, see the pollution of God's creation and the architectural horrors of postwar prosperity, to know without doubt which epoch this really was.

Now the train pulled into a volcanically soot-encrusted shop filled with steam-puffing, smoke-belching locomotives. This sudden, immediate, oppressive anachronism could persuade one to believe in the illusion of a journey out of time. Most of the passengers probably welcomed it. They expected this no-man's-land between yesterday and today. The stratospheric weightlessness of stepping out of the present was the main event on the bill.

But he was gravely affected by it. There was no past. There

was only perpetual present. Today suddenly acquired a reality that ate up yesterday. Nothing of the elegant fin de siècle or the winning Jazz Age was left. What had been resurrected from that time was what had once been heavy, dark, and ominous. Each horror of the present had been in bud then. The curse was an old one: All who survived would suffer humanity's guilt; no pleasure would remain unspoiled, no promise believable. Nothing could be taken easily that had once been taken easily; nothing could be indulged now that had once been savored thoughtlessly. The brutal man of today had incubated in the innocent boy of that time. Like Narcissus, he had seen his reflection, and it was his fall.

Gone too was any indulgence with which he might have looked back on his adventure with the woman in the turban. Only the horror was still alive. She'd finally managed to get them to complete the act, after an hour of coaxing and maternal soothing for which he'd been grateful then but which for years afterward—and especially right now—had tormented him. Even worse was the memory of her encouraging cries once she'd lodged him firmly in the saddle. However many layers of happier life-truths might since have settled over this one, they didn't count. The Sphinx in Paris had affirmed that his Christian-pious dread of the Black Hole was nothing but superstition. Not to mention the following decades, and the long-as-a-freight-train procession of girlfriends. The blackness frightened him no longer. There were at least as many dark girls as blondes of all shades, even a few carrot-red ones, among the women in his life; but he'd always punished deception severely. None of this had reconciled him. Now, once more in the presence of the fifteen-year-old who had sidled into the life of the sixty-five-year-old, he knew that his basic fright had never left him.

That, and on top of it the thought of Linda—and Denise—did not augur well for the forthcoming copulation with the Finnish woman from the tribe of illusion-purveying travel agents. It was not conducive even to raising it to the level of a tourist's luxury-class dream. Myths and legends had driven the fifteen-year-old boy on—"*Into the sleeping compartment of the millionaire arms dealer Sir Basil Zacharoff storms a noble Spanish lady on her honeymoon who has fled from her new husband. Sir Basil protects her; she spends the night with him, leaves her unloved husband, and becomes Lady Zacharoff*"—but the myths had evaporated. Things like that didn't happen anymore, not even in Disneyland.

And yet he was still not prepared to renounce the forthcoming event. The sleepwalk through life continued.

W HILE THE TRAIN halted in Milan, he washed the afternoon's sweat from his body in the stylistically perfect but far too small washbasin. ("It's a scandal there are no showers on this train!" But in the days of the old Orient-Express one hadn't showered. One used small pads of cotton soaked in eau de cologne; his aunts had laid in a plentiful supply of them. And he'd had to promise never to remove his gloves, except at table of course, or if an adult deigned to shake his hand.)

Just as then, he now changed for dinner. But he wasn't playing the make-as-though game ironically enough, so it was only the dark suit, not a dinner jacket. Even that seemed to him a spooky disguise. What in New York was a daily, automatic routine seemed contrived here, an action prompted by the dictates of some obscure and shady purpose—

He suddenly remembered a walk he'd taken with Denise one fine morning. It had been some brief holiday in the middle of the week, hardly worth going to the pioneer house in Southampton; Linda had gone off somewhere to demonstrate against Russian atrocities in Afghanistan, and he'd been free for the ecstatic Denise. They strolled through Central Park and on Fifth Avenue. The steps in front of the Metropolitan Museum were as usual covered with a motley array of people looking like participants in a pseudo-folklore tramps' ball. What are all these people doing, hanging around art treasures, Denise wondered, "like beggars in front of a church." He was about to answer that this was indeed a kind of church: a temple of culture. Nowadays on Sunday morning, educated people went to a museum rather than to church. But he skipped that remark and started giving her a description of the time just before the outbreak of the black death in London as he had learned it from some vivid presentation in a school book. Then too the whole world had lamented the fall from piety and God's grace; it had been a period of constant festivity, when everyone had dressed up crazily, all sorts of healers had preached, all sorts of nomads had appeared on the scene—quacks and street-corner prophets, stargazers, phony monks, magicians, ascetics—and people flocked to them. Fanatical brotherhoods and sects were formed while overnight the number of rats in the city multiplied alarmingly. . . .

Denise clutched his arm so tightly that he hastened to assure her that he knew today's reality better than most and therefore did not share the insidious doomsday mood that overshadowed life with a sense of fearful brevity and meaninglessness: the top topic of Linda's pals. But even as he talked to her in this comforting vein, the contrary conviction impressed itself on him, although he didn't say as much. It was indeed so, the world really was becoming senile, preparing to die; in the general masquerade and flight from the present, in the addiction of glorifying the past, wearing its old clothes, retrieving its discarded objects, reviving outlived life-forms, there was concealed a gallows humor. Somehow it was known that these rags, this junk, these attitudes were an as-if that was merely replacing some other as-if and might be just as easily replaced in turn by yet another as-if. And it was known that the basic reality of existence wasn't changed by whatever as-ifs one happened to clothe it in, whatever fiction one dressed it up in.

There was certainly one marked difference between those plague-ridden days and today; then, people conceded Death's absolute sovereignty. At every waking moment they looked him straight in the eye, with fear, dread, and respect. Whether he held out the promise of eternal bliss or eternal hell, a resurrection in flesh or a sinking into oblivion, one had him along all through life, beside one, in front of one, within one, the most loyal and dependable of life's companions. Today, people tried to sweep him under the carpet, lived as though Death didn't exist. While the hecatombs piled up to the sky and each day brought an escalating danger that all over the world dying would soon be even more merciless than in the plague days, an outrageous conviction was fermenting that sometime soon Death would be conquered. This was the most dangerous as-if of all.

He cast a last glance in the mirror, thank goodness so small and low that he could check the knot of his tie without being disturbed by the rest of his physiognomy, and thought, I'll probably be laid out in just such a suit as this, with just such a white shirt and somber tie. In the meantime there was nothing to do but bravely to face one's continuing existence; and part of that was the obligation to nourish and reproduce oneself—if only in an as-if.

THE DISTINGUISHED émigré couple from Holland or Switzerland were the only other occupants of the dining car, and they sat with small, well-bred smiles as though unaware of the glittering desolation around them, the bridal splendor of the set tables, the waiters poised in anticipation. They too saw through the masquerade and greeted it with the melancholy humor of those tempered by trial.

The train was on the move again. Milan was behind them, a glowing ember, a faint glimmer in the night, like all the other countless cities of *l'Europe illuminée,* the sight of which might well awaken longing in the breast of a young person today. Dream destinations given to us by kind permission of light bulbs and neon tables. Behind the reflections of the little table lamps and the crystal and silver, dark silhouettes of one of the most beautiful landscapes on earth slid dimly past: the mountains and islands bespattered with cypresses like black torches in the moonlit wedge of metallic smoothness that was Lake Maggiore. Soon they'd be leaving Italy and entering Switzerland— the last citadel of a Europe that had long since surrendered.

He sat down at a table facing the entrance through which the

Finnish woman would come. It was no coincidence that he was thereby almost ostentatiously placed with his back to the distinguished, benignly smiling couple—and he did this out of consideration for them. It was the first time in his life that he'd shown respect for the feelings of others so sensitively, and the thought tickled his sense of irony: Well, well, he said to himself, I'm nothing but a petit bourgeois after all.

Twice he was obliged to disappoint single persons who inquired whether they might sit at his table. It irked him that he had relinquished his freedom of choice. Blind grasping at the first chance was excusable at the age of fifteen, but it was shaming today, except that he had long since concluded that when all was said and done, even the most careful selection was still a coincidence. If now he felt a faint enmity rising in him against the white-blonde Finnish woman, it was only natural; the complacency with which women jumped into a vacuum, blocking the space for others, had always irritated him.

He wondered whether there might ever have been a chance for an inner harmonious agreement to evolve between Linda and him, as between the two old émigrés here. Philemon and Baucis in the dining car of the Orient-Express: it was a contradiction in terms. But the barbarity of his and Linda's living side by side but never together pleased him even less. Perhaps he might free both of them from this disgrace if he were to stop mounting her like a satyr. What about giving up the whole little game? He was sixty-five and entitled to a pension. After a half-century of doggedly fulfilling one's preordained biological function, however, one could not be expected to abstain overnight.

He was on the point of beckoning the waiter to come and take his order when she entered. She had exchanged her linen dress for another equally simple and well-cut one of burgundy-colored raw silk, and was wearing a thick and—to judge from the precious diamond clasp—apparently genuine pearl necklace. An expensive lady, then. Her makeup, discreetly and artfully applied, was more conspicuous than before—perhaps she'd been wearing none at all at their first meeting? She had learned how to put it on as a stewardess on a good airline, he mused. At any rate, she was not, like Denise, herself a beautician.

Nor was she a beauty; but she did have a pleasantly open, intelligent face, if a trifle hard, and she was well built. Her short-cropped white-blonde hair and lightly tanned skin accentuated her trim, athletic body. He admired the forthright way she sat down and ordered a large vodka; so as not to be a drag he ordered one too. At the first sip he realized that the earlier gin and tonics had not been entirely harmless, for he felt the seething of drunkenness pressing at his temples. But it would take far greater quantities of liquor than this to make him really drunk; his entire life he'd forced himself to combat his lack of affection for alcohol by drinking all the more. He ordered a light Italian white wine to go with the first courses and a Bordeaux for the later ones.

She knew something about food and drink too. It amused him to look through the pompous menu with her and let her speculate as to what once innocuous but now no doubt inedible concoctions might be hidden behind the ornate French names. She ate heartily and drank without inhibition, and because the food and wines were better than they had expected, he too ate and drank more than usual. Their conversation was effortless and amusing. He could have kissed her when she told about a dilemma she was in: Her black lover, a Senegalese, for whom she had redecorated her apartment in shades of pink and pistachio green because his dark skin was shown off to best advantage against such a background, had left her, and his successor was a red-haired Irishman. Compared with such an aesthetic problem, Linda's preoccupations seemed pitifully contrived.

"Do you lock the door to your compartment when you go to bed?" he asked.

"It depends," she replied. "For the time being I have no desire to go to sleep."

He liked it too that she turned down his offer of champagne. "I'd rather have it tomorrow morning," she said with an ambiguous smile as they perched once again on stools in the bar, and continued with her lethal shots of vodka. He soon noticed that he'd indulged in too much of a good thing. His was that light, bright, trancelike state in which one's consciousness functions more alertly and more sharply than usual but has ceased to have any influence over one's actions. He was filled with the benignity of total irresponsibility. Just as surely as he was sitting in the fictitious "here" of the saloon car, boozing and chatting with a Finnish woman, as though this runaway fairground ride weren't taking them both to a quite different "there," which would knock down the make-believe situation the way a child would knock down a cardboard cutout and abandon it in favor of another, better game, so too were they all headed full tilt, drunk on the game, careering through space on the planet's carnival ride toward an inscrutable "somewhere else" where every here and now would prove to be sheer fiction. He felt free as never before. Perhaps it was the alcohol, which had liberated him from old hypnotic bonds, or the philosophy he had long nurtured, which let him play a game for his whole life, to give it up now like a child sick of the artifice. Besieged by insoluble problems? Beset by questions to which there were no answers? Not he.

He procrastinated solely on account of this marvelous sense of well-being. Between the burning impatience he'd felt with the turbaned woman and his enthusiasm today lay a span of fifty years. He was enjoying the distance.

They spoke of America. She'd roamed around it doing various jobs, most recently as a travel guide. She told him of a strange experience she'd had while taking a group through Death Valley. They'd left Los Angeles very late, and to everyone's dismay it had grown dark before they were halfway there. The sky had been clear, however, and the desert landscape between snowcapped mountains all the more romantic. But the almost reverent mood of the company changed abruptly when, right in the middle of the fatal valley, miles from any human abode, the bus had a breakdown, some motor defect or other over which the driver—aided, abetted, and sorely hindered by a number of technically well-informed passengers—labored in vain. There was no question of danger; if nobody came by who could inform the highway patrol—it became more and more unlikely that anyone would with each passing minute—the worst that could happen was that they would have to spend the night on the bus.

Night fell with such dramatic force that it chilled the fathers and mothers and their children to the very marrow of their bones. Until then they'd been chatting and joking, walking around to stretch their legs and breathe the pure air. Now they became frightened. For a while it was pitch-dark; only the stars hung hugely in the black firmament, and the mountains looked as if they'd been cut out of it. Then at some point the moon rose behind the snowcapped peaks without showing itself; only its light stole into the valley and took possession of it—"a moonscape," she called it. Bone dry, the desert stretched away in patterns played by milky light and dense black shadow. Sand dunes glistened, stones lay strewn about as though cast there by God's wrath. All this quickly subdued the stranded voyagers. But soon they realized that the scariest element of the primeval landscape was its stillness. They couldn't bear this stillness and did everything to drive it off. They yodeled and whistled, they sang choruses, they improvised a strident orchestra by banging aluminum cans and plucking rubber bands. Finally one of them succumbed—as a joke to begin with, then genuinely and more and more earnestly—to the missionary instinct that apparently slumbers in every true American breast. Flexing his diaphragm and booming in the unctuous tones of a Bible thumper, he addressed God and declared himself ready for the intention that had been revealed to him this day, namely that all sinful mankind must be destroyed, not only those present here in the desert but first and foremost those in the cities who had outrageously dared reach for the sky, the daughters of the whores of Babylon and the others all over the country right down to the farthest, remotest spots, the quietest backwaters, the loneliest farms; the sinners and the depraved were all over and must be wiped out, removed from the face of the blessed earth. . . .

And just as the fanatic's voice was beginning to crack in its shrillness, the motor sprang back to life, God was forgotten in a trice, and whooping obscenities, the travelers drove through the bone-white night to the safety of a motel.

He gazed constantly into her light eyes while she told the story. When she finished he said, "How stupid to interpret stillness as a sign of God's wanting to destroy His creation. It was *because* of the stillness that He invented the whole circus." She seemed first uncomprehending, then crestfallen. He went on, "God's afraid of silence Himself," and she continued to look at him, her face open, cleansed of everything that wasn't the real her. "He abhors silence because it's against His creation. But whoever has experienced it truly must hate the hullabaloo. It started with the Big Bang and will probably be an even bigger racket after this wretched planet has been finally, irrevocably destroyed." He groped for words, conscious of how drunk he was. "Today we can't really do with a crucified man as the paradigm of human suffering. I propose an alternative: Beethoven, who was granted deafness but who was still obliged to listen within himself to all that God was able to pit against the stillness. . . ."

She remained silent. He continued to gaze into her eyes, then took her hand and said, "I know, I know, I'm talking nonsense. I think we ought to drink another tiny glass of this vodka."

Her face was so open that in his crystal-clear drunkenness, which registered everything more sharply than usual, he felt himself falling headlong into it. The train thundered along a series of curves. Sometimes the rock faces on both sides of the track came so close that the gleam and glare of the brightly illuminated train flew back and spilled out above them. The piano's tinkling became shrill in these narrow gulches. Foaming waterfalls swished past silently. The bar and the tables with the little lamps were now filled. He didn't care at all whether the people sitting around them were complete strangers or the passengers he already counted as acquaintances, so to speak, such as the émigré couple and the American visionary and his nail-hard Eurasian wife and the three generations of globe-trotting Britons. He was here, with her opposite him, removed from the world, isolated in exclusive twosomeness. He existed only in her face.

It had always been in the face of a woman that the unfulfillable promise had appeared to enslave him. Even the most attractive girls at the Sphinx had left him cold if there was no signal exchanged when he first looked at them, some sign that they had an agreement—not always positive, sometimes even hostile, but always some kind of a mutual cognizance, or recognition rather, seeing oneself in the other's eyes. Perhaps this was why he liked to gain power over women's faces by watching how they disintegrated in the spasms of orgasm, how they were destroyed by passion. Seldom had he seen a sign of bliss in the wave of agony and lust flooding a woman's face at the instant when she came, and only very rarely (for which reason he'd once, long, long ago, idolized Linda) had he seen the melting into another kind of rapturous surrender, the unreserved rushing into his eyes—the face of love.

He pulled her up by the hand. "Come on."

As her compartment was in a car in front of the dining car, and his behind, they had to part. Her hand slipped from his.

He felt insecure, weaving along on rubbery legs, thankful that it might be attributed to the shaking of the train. The pianist went on tickling the ivories; he reached the end of his repertoire and started all over again with the Blue Danube waltz; "C'est Si Bon" was on its way. The mood was festive and generously hospitable, friendships had been struck up all around. His departure, which surely could mean only one thing, as he had been seen in the company of only one person the entire evening, seemed to him like running a gantlet through the horde of randily affable drunks. The walk through the narrow corridor of the next car seemed as long as a trek between two desert oases.

Just as he was navigating across the gyrating platform to the next car, he stumbled smack into the idiot German boy and his mother. She was wearing a dressing gown and was in a condition of acutely confused embarrassment, indeed on the point of tears. She drove the huge, ill-starred child along in front of her with scarcely disguised violence and desperation, while he showed nothing but cherub-cheeked lack of comprehension of the malheur that had overtaken him in his sleep. She had bound a towel around his pajama pants, and she held up the tail of his silk dressing gown on high, as a bridesmaid holds a bridal train. She seemed to view the besmirching not only as evidence of a painfully hopeless lack of control on the part of her unfortunate son but as a social affront, there on this luxury train, a soiling of the prewar prestige under whose banner they were traveling. The stench was quite as penetrating and earthy as the boy's eyes—sky blue, peering, turned up at the corners like Mona Lisa's smile—were enigmatic and otherworldly.

Prompted by some involuntary instinct, he clicked open the door to the toilet and—like the chivalrous Empire-and-Commonwealth Briton—held it open until mother and son could pull it to from the inside, staring all the while into the middle distance like a well-trained lackey so as to avoid her grateful eyes that sought his understanding.

Once safely in his compartment, he let himself fall on the bunk and tugged at his tie. Struggling clumsily to free himself of his jacket, he realized just how drunk he must be, but he was more fascinated by the thought that the idiot boy's silk dressing gown was a twin to the one he would now don to commence his journey to the platinum-blonde Finnish woman's bed. And then it occurred to him that he'd forgotten to ask her for the number of her compartment. It was unlikely that she could come to his, situated as she was way up front beyond the saloon car and the dining car, where things were still in full swing.

166

What a completely absurd situation. They had parted at the bar in a lovers' trance, with the slow relinquishing of hands and long looks that two people indulge in when they part enthralled with each other and expect their spellbound leave-taking to lead to a rapturous reunion. The list of passengers provided by the Orient-Express company lay on his night table, but it offered no solution to the conundrum. He could guess that from the list of names of women traveling alone—Ms. Hobson, Ms. Kowalski, Ms. Lund, and Mrs. Millard-Herbert—she was likely to be the third, but there were no compartment numbers indicated with the names. She was an experienced travel guide and would have enough know-how to ascertain his whereabouts—that was a faint but buoyant hope. But now the whole thing was nothing but a besotted interlude, a tragicomedy fizzling out in a completely trivial whimper.

This made him furious. He was not inclined to give up so easily. He needed a woman and he needed one right now. He'd not had one since Honolulu, which, in view of his sexual appetite, was an immense period of abstinence. There was also a soft inner voice to be shouted down, which kept whispering that his purported blundering might be a providential expedient, that he had been in danger of letting himself in for more than just another copulative joust. Serenely banal as all indubitable truths must be, the warning towered there before him: he was now spared the disillusionment that would have been the inevitable result of such an undertaking of the soul, if not tonight then tomorrow. Even the basest of his youthful adventures had contained a whiff of this—a rabid fervor, for instance, with which the woman in the silver-gray silk turban had instructed him on the whereabouts of her compartment, pressing up against him in the accordion-bellows at the platforms of the adjacent cars, scythed and unscythed like two broad scissors blades beneath their feet, urging him with her smoky voice and routine kisses into which his prim mouth sank as into a volcanically seething morass. . . .

Thus was the spirit willing but the flesh too strong. His body craved sexual activity. He reminded himself that someone who never tired of denouncing nature's eternally futile fertility lived in existential contradiction if he so eagerly obeyed the call of blind procreation; and sarcasm did not enhance the weak excuses. But this did nothing to relieve his present need. Of course, there were various ways to divest oneself of the loathsome viscous juice whose accumulation caused this craving. True, one couldn't trick nature by spilling one's seed, for one did that anyway in nine hundred ninety-nine cases out of a thousand, regardless of whether one employed a woman for the enterprise or not. Look at his marriage to Linda, for example. The strange thing was that the abstraction and ultimate bypassing of the natural expedient, woman or man, sublimated the act, as though in doing so one came closer to the abstinence of the saints.

He remembered his youth, the time before he fell into the trap of the woman in the silver-gray turban. The sexual urge had had him in its grip even more than at this moment. Of course he had given in to the vice of adolescence so cruelly denounced by his aunts that its punishment would not only be eternal condemnation to hellfire but also to blindness in lifetime. Yet he felt that those days of doubt and fear had been more innocent, cleaner than the ones that followed after his fall in the Orient-Express and were crowned by his frequent visits to the 'Sphinx,' not to speak of all later years.

Thinking fondly of Denise's nanny hand, he reached down and tried to imagine what she might feel when she touched his swelling, not just as a foretaste of the delights it held in store for her, but also in her effort to identify with him, to find out just what it was he was feeling. What else was love but an attempt at identification, after all? . . . He thought also of Linda; and the idea that she might snap out of her erotic lethargy and enjoy, even delight, in this effort to enter another's being, brought his blood to the seething point. Soon his prudishly suppressed erotic fantasies were liberated, and he missed the corn-blonde Finnish woman not a moment more.

The train thundered along its rails, by now most likely glinting in the moonlight. The wheels beat time relentlessly, a beat that surely must reduce the tinkling of the piano, presumably still prevalent in the bar, to sheer negligibility—

. . . the memory of one of Linda's cocktail parties shot through his head. An intellectual with a Schopenhauer brow set in a mane of white hair that resembled a dandelion's fluffy ball of seed had bored him to the point of defecation in expounding a thesis on the strange concept of "Promethean shame." Only with considerable effort could he listen at all, for the erudite gentleman had been eating onions and his breath was even less tolerable than the aggressive tenor of his cultural pessimism. The thoughts of the philosopher whom the man quoted were convincing, however. The sense of inadequacy, of inferiority in comparison with the ever more perfect machinery man now employed must lead to a new kind of shame. What brain could measure up to a computer? What athlete keep up with a motorcycle? The grandiloquence of the future-dreaming Texan at the bar who saw himself as a visionary in control of the cosmos, thanks to modern technology, was counterbalanced by the deep if unacknowledged certainty that humanity, compared with its machines, was a pitiful worm. . . .

. . . and yet these machines were definitely a divine glorification, or to be blunt, an idolization of the job that had caused man to build them in the first place, the commission to destroy nature in the course of creating another one, an abstract sidereal space-nature whose dimensions stretched to infinity and gave accommodation to termites rather than *Homo sapiens*. . . .

. . . the Promethean shame of today's humanity corresponded nicely to the mood of inadequacy in which our forebears threw themselves down before the craven image of a gigantic, volcanically ejaculating lingam. . . .

. . . these fleeting thoughts too were pulled back into the purple of his present feelings, and his consciousness blacked out, as the charging locomotive let out a shrill scream into the night.

* * *

ACCORDING TO THE BROCHURE, high on the list of the Orient-Express's fancy features stood the promise of a short early-morning stop in Lausanne in order to take on freshly baked croissants for breakfast. When he'd read this in Venice he'd asked himself who might still be naive enough to attend such an event as though it were a ceremonial occasion. It turned out that the majority of the passengers were doing just that, for when he awoke in full daylight and stuck his throbbing head into the corridor, all the other compartment doors were already wide open and the occupant birds had flown to breakfast. A glance at his wristwatch told him nothing but the infuriating truth that his eyes were aging; he was unable to read the phantom digits and was far too groggy to reckon the difference between Tokyo time and Western European time anyway.

He looked out the window. The train slid slowly through a scene of destruction such as surrounds all cities today: the jagged edges of villagelike suburbs, building sites waiting to be coated with concrete; garbage dumps; huts with towel-sized vegetable plots; depots behind whose fences wolfhounds raced along, barking furiously at the train. Behind it all, the city, soaking in its haze, gray now, abstract, not a vestige of promise anywhere. Only as the train passed a small station without stopping did he catch sight of the word PARIS, followed by a blurred suffix denoting some precinct.

They were circumnavigating Paris on the equivalent of a ring road, and mixed with his annoyance at its being so late there arose in him, like an echo from the distant past, a silly, youthful disappointment: the train must have halted at the Gare de Lyon while he was still asleep, and he'd missed the chance to get out, stretch his legs, buy a newspaper, and look around as he'd done as a fifteen-year-old—and also to enjoy being seen as a passenger of the Orient-Express. The myth of the luxury train was wedded to the myth of Paris, the one as threadbare and as indestructible as the other. Both were components in the myth of an erstwhile Europe whose far-flung brilliance (including the glory of the Royal and Imperial Austro-Hungarian Monarchy and a colorful spate of derivative states) had been joined to the bejeweled and beggar-ridden fairy-tale world of the Ottoman Empire (or what was left of it) by this very train. This myth was based in facts, after all, however pixilated they seemed today. Today's world lacked this factual quality. It was a world of make-believe. Paris was now as abstract as befitted its existence between two phantoms—belonging just as much to the Jazz Age and the Belle Époque as to the American visionary's space-nature.

And belonging also to nothing at all; belonging to both solely in its fancy-dress getup, in its gesture. The refurbished and reinstated Orient-Express linked no realms of fairy-tale reality. Twice a week it commuted leisurely between the interim abstraction of the Occident and a Byzantine ersatz in the form of unreal Venice, purposely anachronistic; a shuttle through a never-never world, a vehicle provided by some ironic courtesy to enable one to sleepwalk through an existence that lacked a proper present.

It was a gray day. Nothing enticed him to sleepwalk for the moment. The end of the line was at hand. He washed and shaved with special care, as on a morning after a dirty night, and took special care to avoid looking directly at his face in the mercifully tiny mirror above the basin. More than the foul dry taste in his mouth and the persistent seething sensation in his ears, an uncomfortable feeling of having made an ass of himself in more ways than one brought back the memory of events of the previous evening. He swallowed a blood pressure pill, then packed his things. Soon they'd be in Calais and would roll aboard the ferry, then switch in Dover to the English continuation of the Orient-Express, which would take them to London. Protected by the armor of his charcoal-gray double-breasted suit, he left his compartment and worked his way along to the dining car.

It was worse than he'd bargained for. The car was full of

passengers, a second sitting, a sumptuous brunch buffet by now laid on. They appeared to have healthy appetites, and the atmosphere recalled a champagne breakfast winding up a festive carnival night. Harsh daylight made banal what the bevy of lamps had romanticized the night before. He plucked up courage and marched as briskly as he could to the only vacant seat. Even if the Finnish woman had been at one of the tables, he could have passed without noticing her or appearing impolite in ignoring her. But there was no sign of her anywhere, thank God.

He was uncomfortably aware of how boorishly he was behaving. He had no idea how to face her. Surely the safest thing would be to act as if nothing had happened between them, but that would also be the coarsest. To laugh and admit his bungling, and then lay part of the blame for the miscarriage of their plan at her doorstep didn't seem advisable either, for it would give her a perfect chance to retort that if there was such a plan it must have been his alone; women were mercilessly quick on the draw when they wanted to hurt or take revenge. Or worse, it would establish a plot between them that might lead to their making up for what they'd missed.

He didn't feel his head was clear enough to analyze the spontaneous horror this last thought aroused in him. It would be a truly sinful moral lapse, for one thing because of Linda, whom he'd betrayed for the first time the previous evening—emotionally, that is, in the willingness of his soul—and for another because of his new spiritual condition, which had come about during the night—if not innocence then chastity: a peculiar kind of chastity but chastity, all right; the chastity of eremites, perhaps of saints. This presumption didn't strike him as absurd. Nor was he ashamed of his pubescent attitude; on the contrary, he was filled with a sense of defiant boyish pride.

It didn't bother him that at least a dozen of his fellow travelers must have seen him holding hands with the Finnish woman and chatting her up like a Levantine traveling salesman and that they now saw him here again, alone and gray-faced at a mid-morning snack that was his tardy breakfast. Last night's fiasco was written all over him, he had no doubt; women especially had an eye for judging whether a man had acquitted himself honorably or not. He remembered that at the beginning of his marriage with Linda, when she had wanted a child but had had difficulty conceiving, they had consulted a gynecologist who determined one particular twenty-four-hour period as being Linda's most susceptible phase, when he, the husband, would be expected to peak in performance of his marital duty. He did his best. In the morning Linda went off to the doctor while he slept it off. He was wakened by a ringing phone: it was Linda relaying the doctor's instructions that he should go posthaste to a laboratory to have his sperm analyzed. When the rather pretty assistant handed him a little earthenware pot and ushered him into a timbered cubicle where he was required to make his offering, the strain was almost too great for him, but with a superhuman effort he finally brought it off. Then, out on the street once more—he proceeded a little way on foot, in order to feel his way gradually back to ordinary life—he saw in the face of every female creature who crossed his shaky path, from an ancient crone to a ten-year-old girl, even a stray cat, the instinctive respect for a fellow who's withstood the ultimate test. He wore the circles under his eyes like medals.

But here, in the midst of the festivity prevailing all around him as the train hastened across French rivers and through French forests on its way to the coast, he felt above such evaluation, no matter where it came from—as long as it wasn't the Finnish woman herself, that is. He was protected by the talisman of his new existential mood, as though his being had been cleansed of impurities. By gratifying his base desire with his own hand he had mocked Nature's commands. In this one respect, at least, he did not want to continue to belong to the zoological species that was meant to breed and multiply in order to destroy God's world.

He didn't ask himself how much of this sentiment could be

ascribed to still undigested experiences of his youth, flotsam from a shipwreck of his tender inner credo, his inextinguishable longing for something he could believe in. In trying to achieve the condition of love the day before, he believed he had aimed at something on the other side—a vanishing point in infinity where all perspectives join together. That this metaphysical aspiration had not terminated in an erotic act, as was usually the case, made him truly grateful. Denise's nanny hand, guided by his own, had sublimated the carnal instincts, which soiled all that was pure, into immaculate abstraction.

Anyway, he felt free enough to get up and help himself to a glass of wine and a slice of smoked salmon from the abundance of hors d'oeuvres and salads on the buffet, even though the mere thought of either made his stomach lurch.

LINDA HAD LOST the child she longed for so badly, and he couldn't think back on her disappointment without experiencing acute physical pain. The loss bound him all the more closely to her since she had been told she could not hope to have another child. She never mentioned it again, but he knew well what it meant to her; from then on she could not sleep with him pleasurably, yet she was inextricably joined to him. This dichotomy aroused his compassion, but she was one of those people who under such circumstances train an innate obduracy to be even harder. He wished, for her sake, that she could love—not him necessarily, but love at all, someone else's child, or a dog for that matter. . . . What we need, he thought, is not so much to be loved as to be able to love—

He felt he'd played a disgraceful game with the blonde the night before. What if she had fallen for his hazardous gamble and had herself come to the point of loving him? It might have been a gift for a while, but could it have led anywhere other than to a second Denise setup? He was doubly relieved at the outcome of his adventure—to stay with the vernacular of the Orient-Express brochure. Still, he'd have been much happier knowing she'd gotten off in Paris.

But she hadn't. He saw her—in a mirror, thank God, which spared him the direct sight of her, as Perseus had been spared that of the Gorgon—when he returned to his seat with his plate of smoked salmon. She must have seen him when he came in. She was sitting with three men at a table on which stood several bottles of liquor. The men were of that type of robust young Englishman who wears his hair combed down in thick bangs over his forehead and ears, like a stage wig. They were all in high spirits, laughing and chatting ebulliently. He had to admit that the young men suited her. He tried to comfort himself with the near-certain supposition that they were all in the travel business, but they had more in common than that: they all belonged to another generation and therefore to a world entirely different from his own, to a different species of humanity, a different planet almost—

And he had to think that at this point Denise might interpolate that love could bridge the distance between any two stars—a moving thought, even more so because in her case it was apparently true and because he himself had wanted to undertake something similar the night before; now it seemed to him more likely to find reality in the Texan's visions.

The salmon on his plate disgusted him. And as he raised his glass and sipped his wine, things went from bad to worse. The mood surrounding him became more and more convivial. He stood up and started back to his compartment. She didn't look up, but one of her new—or old, perhaps?—companions raised his eyes as he passed their table.

In the corridor two cars down—where the German couple with the idiot child were quartered—he was startled by the harsh sound of an amplified voice. The management of the train regretted to announce that a change of plans had been necessary. The English railwaymen were on strike, and it was thus impossible for the train to cross from Calais to Dover. Instead the passengers would take the ferry from Boulogne and complete the journey to London by bus.

He nodded as he heard this. Quite in keeping. The dream

journey ends with a rude awakening. He entered his compartment almost ecstatically. There it was, palely let into the blond paneling: the small medallion that had recalled the mood of his youth for one long moment and lured him on this trip. He was grateful that it had. The reason why had become clear.

OUT IN FRONT of the window, the countryside lost its charm. The weather too deteriorated; strips of gray clouds came in low and quickly from the Channel; wind plucked at the sparse bushes beside the tracks. The train slowed down and then drew into the towering gallery walls of the Boulogne ferry dock. At a walking pace the dream vehicle had reached its destination. Gazing out of the window, he watched the passengers swarm out into the concrete desert—it was on the tip of his mind-tongue to call them his "partners in karmic crime"—the Texas clairvoyant to the fore, padding dutifully behind his striding Eurasian spouse. The Empire-building Britons were there too. Neither the idiot child nor his parents were present; perhaps they had gotten off in Paris so that the boy might take in the Louvre. He couldn't spot the Finnish woman either, but he did catch sight of the gentle émigré couple. They both wore that expression peculiar to people who have endured a grueling test. They too seemed satisfied with what they'd experienced.

When the youthful steward with the protruding ears had taken charge of his valise, he gave him a tip whose size brought crimson blood rushing to the lad's cheeks. Perhaps the steward would consider it an act of senility, he thought to himself. When, as a boy all those years before, he'd given the conductor a tip that was too big, the man's ironical look had made it clear that he put it down to inexperience and a desire to show off. He turned back into the empty compartment, now discreetly anonymous. The Art Deco intarsia was even paler, light-years away, set in the mirror-blank paneling. He thought to himself, That belongs to the archaeological side of art history. To the new species of humanity it must appear as strange and illegible as a hieroglyph in a Mayan temple. He wondered whether God, whose sole concern it was to keep his myriad creatures going at all costs, did in fact notice just what manner of little games they invented to fill the void of their existence. Or was he content to count the stars in the *Guide rouge?* . . .

He left the train. He could smell the seaweed on the summer wind blowing in gusts around the maze of concrete walls. He joined his partners in crime as they climbed the stairs to another level, where, rumor had it, there were a bar and a restaurant. From a caged gallery that ran along the side of a wall like a catwalk in a prison, he gazed down through the mesh at the forsaken navy-blue train with the shining brass letters COMPAGNIE INTERNATIONALE DES WAGONS-LITS and the golden emblems VENICE–SIMPLON–ORIENT-EXPRESS adorning the freshly lacquered cars. Against this stark background it looked anachronistic and yet, in an excruciating, uncomfortable way, up-to-date, like a Sullivan-style Stalinist bureaucratic palace in the midst of the jerry-built wastes of East Berlin. But that's no longer Disneyland! he thought to himself excitedly. I must tell Linda at once. Americanik is passé; the style of Europe's new age is being dictated from some other quarter.

The herd quickly filled the bare waiting room, no different from any of the other tourist mobs that wandered in the tens and hundreds of thousands like gypsies through the culture-satiated ruins of the Occident. The promised restaurant turned out to be a bar. The passengers all blinked asininely, like extras on a film set being told that one scene has been completed and they must settle back to wait for the next. Their affected jolly solidarity started to break up. Individual initiatives became evident; one man studied timetables, although under the circumstances this was quite superfluous. And now he noticed the Finnish woman with her new cronies. She was obviously good at dealing with such situations, and seemed to be in the best of spirits as she led her companions to the bar, where she succeeded in organizing beer and brandy. Most of the other passengers were grouped on or around the utilitarian seats, doing nothing but waiting.

They were waiting for *him* who would sooner or later be sure

177

to appear: the shepherd. He duly arrived, in the form of a master of ceremonies of such ludicrous proportions that one surmised he had been shot over from Disneyland in answer to the emergency. In which of old Europe's many trashcans could the Orient-Express company have found him, and for which special effect in their extensive public relations had they trained him—decked out in a richly braided coffee-brown dress coat and with an admiral's cocked hat perched on his great tomcat head, with bristling moustachios and beer-yellow muttonchops swept high over his cheeks, he looked like a mixture between a hotel hall porter and a circus director. Standing squarely on a ramp and speaking in a fruity voice with a quaint homespun accent and a smart military rasp, in which could be detected the unconditional trustworthiness of a veteran campaigner, he welcomed the company on behalf of the management and seemed also to be offering personal apologies on behalf of the prime minister for the untimely strike, the "dastardly delay, and the damnable discomfort." With the studied pathos of a practiced after-dinner speaker and the facility of a carnival barker, he then proceeded to announce the itinerary: everyone would have to be patient for a short while longer, he regretted, the ferry was even later than expected, but despite a rather strong wind for this time of year he trusted that the crossing would be pleasant. Tiresome customs procedure in Dover stipulated that each passenger present his baggage personally, unfortunately; although there were no porters and, also, only a very limited number of handcarts, the personnel would, of course, do everything in their power to help. Once on the ferry there would be a bar in a specially cordoned-off portion of the upper deck where drinks would be dispensed free of charge.

From the direction of the counter, where the Finnish woman was knocking them back with her long-haired buddies, there came an enthusiastic round of applause.

H E   S T O O D at the rail of the ferry, packed with young homecoming tourists. The array of their colorful parkas reminded him of rows of loaves of sugar-coated gingerbread at a fair-ground stall. He felt drained and rendered helpless by their un-bounded energy; adolescents at best, yet already masters of this ship, this world, this age. They were children of the small folk of a prosperous epoch that—if it lasted—would grant them in turn a prosperous small-folk existence. Their self-confidence was astonishing. In none of them could he detect any sign of pubescent anxiety. Well, of course. Sexual problems were as good as unknown to them, and religious ones only in isolated cases. The longing for fulfillment in wholeness, the torment of being unable to communicate, the craving to break out of the solitude of godforsaken individuality was all limited to politics in their case. They were inundated from all sides with offers that promised prompt and definite solutions. Those who went on suffering despite all this could seek solace from a psychiatrist.

There was nothing left to be seen of the French coastline but a dirty blue smear above the heaving gray water, and the gulls that had escorted the ferry in an aerial dance had fallen back. A very young blonde, still almost a child, was standing at the rail of the deck below him. One end of the red silk scarf she wore around her neck was flapping in the wind. It was a signal that made his heart sing. Was such a sign universal and comprehensible at all times? Not damned to transience? Not eternally en-coded and withdrawn to a planetary distance like the Mayan hieroglyph or the medallion in the blond paneling of a phony train, speaking only to those who inhabited the same realm of space? . . . Kitty was close at hand, she whom he'd not seen since the summer in the Dobrudja. Thank God, he told himself; that adventure too had come to an immaculate close.

Where was the Finnish woman? The Orient-Express passengers were roped into an enclosure around the bar, and she would be there with her hirsute consorts. He discovered her sitting at a table within easy reach of the divine source, and he now felt collected enough to go over and bid her adieu. Intent on making his approach somewhat more elegant, he went to the bar and ordered an espresso, and only then turned in her direction and made as though he'd just caught sight of her. She looked over at him. He smiled; she responded, broadly, gaily, easily. He went to her table. "Won't you join us in a glass?" she asked thickly, slurring her consonants. She held up her glass in front of him. Her hand was ugly; the malignantly twinkling little diamonds on her rings made it seem almost cruel. Not a comforting nanny hand at all. There was nothing of the alertness of the previous evening in her eyes, only the dull glaze of a tippler; it evoked sympathy in him. He thanked her for the offer to drink from her glass, nodded to her cronies, bent down, and gently kissed her forehead. For a moment her face was turned up to him with a questioning, expectant expression. It was the face of a woman on the threshold of age. A dime-a-dozen life had been spent there and now had no future. A faceless face, he thought to himself. As he straightened up he could see from the roots of her hair that she was probably a genuine blonde, not a bottle one. No, she had not disappointed him. He stroked her cheek gently and went back to his place at the railing.

From a point somewhere behind him the storybook Britons suddenly appeared: grandfather elephant hunter, grandmother crumbling pillar of the Imperium, son Rolls-Royce salesman, grandson dream-walker. Like a family of ducks they waddled purposefully toward the ship's prow as though set on hopping straight across to their beloved island. *They were coming home.*

Again he looked down to the lower deck, but the girl with the red scarf had disappeared. I was forever being led close to the truth, he said to himself, but never was I allowed to discover it fully. The truth! It was hidden in the stillness, audible only for the pure, the genuinely blond.

Just as he was turning his eyes toward the chalk cliffs of Dover, there occurred a tremor in the interior of his brain, ever so gentle and yet alarmingly violent, as though a string had broken there. For a split second he was unconscious, no longer of this world, taken out of life; then his consciousness returned, almost clearer than it had been before. This left him filled with a sense of wonderment, but there was no need to ask himself what it meant; the message could not be wrongly construed. He carefully tested his face muscles to see whether any part of them had gone dead. They reacted normally to his commands, as did his arms and legs.

The time had come, he thought. Now we shall soon embark on the last, only truly great adventure. The adventure we seek throughout our lives, above all in carnal knowledge and in love. Now it's time to enter the Black Hole that gobbles everything up and regurgitates it, in the eternal process of maintaining business as usual. What it looked like in there couldn't be conjectured. Stillness would reign at last, probably. But all this one would find out. The mere passage of time would prove it.

He peered at his wristwatch, saw once more only the spooky black numbers wriggling against the gray background. He didn't bother to put on his glasses and transpose Tokyo time to its Greenwich equivalent—I live beyond the one and the other, he thought to himself, no matter how little of it is left me. He unfastened the watch from his wrist and cast it into a wave that foamed up around the hull and then returned whence it came.

## End of Journey